LOST SONS
The Fall of New Atlantis

Greg Ballan

Hadrosaur Productions, Mesilla Park, NM

Lost Sons: The Fall of New Atlantis
Hadrosaur Productions
First Edition: February 2025

Copyright © 2025 Greg Ballan
Cover Art Copyright © 2025 Laura Givens

ISBN-13: 979-8-9851120-9-2

Hadrosaur Productions
P.O. Box 2194
Mesilla Park, NM 88047-2194
www.hadrosaur.com

To my amazing girlfriend, Amy Wilcox. You've supported me and believed in me when I doubted myself the most. This work is dedicated to you. Thank you for being the wind in my sails through the stormy seas and darkest waters.

Acknowledgments

Creating a story is not a task done by the author alone; at least not for me. I pick people's brains, chat annoyingly and endlessly about characters, plot points and motivations to anyone who's patient enough to endure my rantings for more than a few minutes. God blessed me with an amazing son, Thomas. He has been my inspiration, sounding board and silent partner. We've spent countless hours at the local coffee shop bantering back and forth how this story should play out … happy ending, tragic ending … being true to the overall themes etc. No writer has ever been blessed with such an amazing and insightful muse. Thomas, this story would never be without your encouragement and patience as I prattled on over multiple cups of Honey Dew iced coffee and hours of conversation.

Also, where would I be without my amazing editor, publisher and most importantly, dear friend and brother in writing, David Lee Summers? David, you have been such a great mentor, you've made this story sparkle like a brilliant diamond. I am forever grateful for your wisdom, guidance and friendship. Thank you for giving me the opportunity to bring *Lost Sons: The Fall of New Atlantis* to life.

LOST SONS
The Fall of New Atlantis

Greg Ballan

The End of a Kingdom

Rivers of scarlet blood stained the snow-covered battlefield. The frenzied clash of steel striking steel and the brittle snap of breaking bone accentuated the banshee wails of the wounded and dying. Through all the madness of battle, the warrior king fought on. Desperation fueled each sword stroke and parry. The scent of blood, sweat and defecation – the all too familiar smells of combat – assaulted his nose with every breath. He watched his own likeness cut down a barbarian with one mighty swing of his ancestral blade and follow up the swing with a thrust into another invader's stomach, disemboweling him. It was him but it wasn't!

Madness! It must be! No man can be in two places at once!

The blow that pierced him came as a surprise. This time, however, the sharp sting from the mortal blow, registered only as a dull pressure as the sharpened steel penetrated his doppelganger's back and burst through his stomach. He watched with detached interest as the barbarian wrenched the blade free from his likeness and held the bloody weapon for all to see. The Nordic king heard the condescending tone of his enemy as the cowardly savage mocked him. He watched as his ghost image gathered the last of his reserves and swung upon his hated foe, he shouted the name of his god, Odin, as his ancestral blade cleaved the enemy's bowels, spilling the steaming guts onto the bloody earth. With his last ounce of strength, he drove his blade into the barbarian chief who'd raided his village and brought death and destruction. Sagahr, the scourge of the north and east had finally met his end. Now he could die an honorable death, his ancestors would welcome him into the hereafter.

He watched his doppelganger fall onto the cool earth; he gazed down at the identical savage wound upon his own torso, probing the gaping hole with a finger. Blood still dripped from the tear in his flesh. The king knew the end had come and welcomed the onrush of death. He waited for the reaper to carry away his soul, eyes wide open, unafraid. He would be with his kin in the land of his ancestors.

A shadow crept over the mountain blotting out the sun, casting a cold gray gloom over the entire battlefield. Those that survived the onslaught fled in fear. He could only watch, helplessly, as his dream *likeness rose up, swallowed in the belly of the shadow. The world went black. The pain ceased. He no longer felt blood warm his flesh and the frozen earth beneath him. His god, Odin, had come for him.*

The Clan Chief, Duncan Kord, opened his eyes, blinking several times adjusting to the alien surroundings.

"Not a dream," he whispered. The battle had been fought. He'd suffered a killing blow. But he'd killed Sagahr, hopefully his people would be able to go on and keep a firm grip on their territory.

"Is this what awaits me beyond death?" Wary eyes studied the exotic surroundings. A rainbow of light illuminated the area around him. The walls of the chamber glowed, pulsing with a steady rhythm. The small device next to him emitted a pale, yellow luminescence and he reached toward it. Kord expected to feel the comforting warmth of heat as he had from several fires. There was no heat from this source of light, just pure radiance.

"What manner of wizardry makes light without fire?"

Kord took a moment to study his surroundings. He was lying in a very comfortable bed. Several tubes violated the flesh of his forearms. Strange objects hummed in a constant rhythm while multi-colored lights danced on several surfaces of each object. Kord lifted the covers off of his chest. He prepared himself for the sight of an ugly open wound but instead found only his warm naked flesh, unscathed and unmarked. With a slight exertion he managed to force himself upright, a dull throbbing pain tingled his mid-section, he had indeed been wounded. Had Odin and the other gods healed him? Was this Valhalla, the land of his forefathers?

The Nordic warrior slipped his legs out from under the covers and with some effort managed to stand upright. He crouched slightly, his body adopting a defensive position. Keen eyes scanned and scrutinized every detail of his surroundings. He sniffed the air, like the wolf, but could detect no familiar scent. The room was devoid of smell. Kord's spine tingled as fear crept through every fiber of his body. He inhaled deeply with practiced rhythm until he was able to master and control the destructive emotion. He studied his body, probing his torso with his fingers. Half a lifetime of battle scars and bruises no longer told a tale upon him. His flesh was as unmarked as that of a newborn child or some untested scholar. What manner of punishment was this? Each scar and discoloration were badges of honor a warrior wore proudly. He attempted to remove one of the tubes from his forearm, but the device seemed fused into his flesh. The more he pulled upon the tubes the more discomfort he experienced; they were not coming off without a struggle. He decided not to risk injury by ripping the offensive object from his limb, just yet. Kord took several steps, and the flashing objects that held the mysterious tubes floated along with his movements. It was then he noticed one light seemed to mimic the beating of his heart. The clan chief willed his heart rate lower and the pulsing light slowed. As he increased his heart rate, the pulsing light also grew in intensity and pulsed quicker.

"A healing temple of the gods," he murmured in awe. "I am in Valhalla."

"I am Duncan Kord, ancestral grandson of Tiberon Kord, greatest of my forefathers, son of Duncan Kord the first. I pray thee gods of my forefathers - Odin, Thor, Loki - find me worthy of a place among chiefs," Kord shouted.

"There are no gods here, Duncan Kord," a voice responded. "This is not the Valhalla of your legends."

Kord turned, his eyes, focusing on every inch of the room. The voice had come from behind him, but his eyes could detect nothing. The warrior king continued to focus on the vacant space, his mind kept telling him his eyes were wrong. Acute senses felt a presence, but he instinctively knew he was in no danger. He took four slow steps toward the noise's source. The soft footsteps of padded feet along the sterile white floor caught his attention. A brief shimmer of something darted directly in front of a large glowing wall panel. He wasn't alone.

Whatever was in the room with him obviously meant him no harm. The Nordic warrior knew he was in no danger. Whoever or whatever they were had miraculously healed him. If they wanted him dead, they could have just left his corpse on the field of battle.

"I know you're here," Kord whispered. "I may not be able to see you, but you haven't mastered the ability to be completely silent; like this." The Nordic chief walked across the floor in a casual gait, yet his feet seemed to glide and roll upon the white sterile surface making no sound. "I am as naked as the day my mother bore me and have things fused to my flesh, I assure you, I am no threat." He opened his hands in a gesture of peace.

Two forms shimmered into being several feet in front of him. Kord was startled at the abrupt manner of their presence and jumped back slightly. "By Odin, what manner of magic is that?" Two of the tiny beings approached him. They were not much bigger than young boys. Their bodies were thin, almost frail. Their eyes were a dark blue that resembled midnight and their hair seemed as white as a fresh mountain snowfall.

"Forgive our deception," they spoke in unison. "Several of the other chosen awoke less peacefully than you did and had to be sedated anew. We trust that will not be necessary in your case."

"Sedated?" Kord asked, not understanding the word.

One of them raised a small object and pressed something on it. A tiny river of blue fluid raced into Kord's forearm before he could react. His body became instantly weak and groggy, his limbs felt encased in granite. Kord stumbled dropping to one knee. He tried to speak but was unable. The thin boy pressed the object one more time and a small trickle of green light flowed from another tube and entered his body. After scant seconds, Kord felt rejuvenated and strong enough to stand again. He exhaled heavily as the bout of weakness passed. Panic shrieked through his body; he was a prisoner. These weren't gods. They were demons from the foulest pit. Would they torture him with weakness and make him a slave puppet for all eternity?

"I am a captive?" Kord studied the clear tubes violating his flesh.

"No, warrior," they said in unison. "We provided you a small taste of the word sedated. Now you comprehend the meaning and it won't be necessary to do this again. You are not a prisoner, but you've been resurrected for a purpose. We are a peaceful society and wish only to live our lives undisturbed and unfettered by the plague of violence and destruction your species is determined to bring upon themselves. Can we trust that you will do no harm and abide by the rules of our society?"

Kord didn't know what to think. By all rights he should be dead. Obviously he wasn't. Maybe this fate was worse. He had no choice, these beings, demons or whatever manner of men could cripple him without raising a weapon. "You have my word, I will obey."

Upon Kord's word, the tubes fused in his arms detached themselves and vanished into the floating objects. The objects drifted to the walls and fused themselves into the structure.

"Again, I am unfamiliar with that word: resurrected," Kord murmured studying his surroundings.

"Healed," both said in unison. "We have given you back your life Duncan Kord, greatest of the clan chieftains. We offer you a new purpose and a chance at a new life. As they spoke, a doorway opened and two more beings entered. These beings were clearly female and Kord became self-conscious about his lack of clothing. The females paid him little attention and simply deposited his clothing and scabbard, then left as quickly and quietly as they had entered. Kord studied his clothing and battle armor. The rips had been repaired perfectly. The bronze and crude steel plates were polished to a mirror sheen. Kord quickly dressed himself and felt somewhat better. He picked up his empty scabbard and looked at his 'Hosts' with suspicion.

"My sword," he stated flatly. "Where is it?"

"Your sword was damaged and is being repaired. It will be re-forged to suit your new purpose. Fret not, warrior, we know how fond your kind is of weapons and we'll not deprive you of your trinket."

"That sword is over two hundred years old, handed down from generation to generation in my bloodline, forged and re-tempered with each passing. It's no mere trinket, demon. It's a symbol of my family's leadership," Kord spat back with vitriol and contempt.

The two frail beings conversed amongst themselves in a language Kord had never heard before while he dressed. After several seconds the one who'd insulted him stepped forward. "It was not my intent to cause offense, Duncan Kord. I offer you my deepest apologies. May we walk and discuss with you why you've been brought here.

"A question first," The Nordic warrior countered, buckling the last strap of his armor.

"What is your inquiry?"

"My wife and my brother were in the front lines of my army. Did they survive?" Kord was unable to conceal the hope and desire contained within his query.

The two slim beings stared at each other for a moment and then sadly looked toward the floor. "They did not survive. Your lands and your people are no more, Duncan Kord."

Kord turned away from them, head bowed in deep sorrow. The battle had no meaning; his death had no meaning. He wasn't dead, yet his brother and wife were in Valhalla. These demons robbed him of eternity with his beloved wife and family; they had cured his wounds and robbed him of his afterlife. A grief-wracked sob escaped him. "Foul demons!" he cursed turning towards the two. "Do you realize what you've done?"

The two beings stepped back, flinching as Kord approached them. They no longer had the means to control the Nordic giant.

"I should be dead, along with my people in Valhalla. You've robbed me of my eternity, my rightful place among my ancestors," Kord spat in a lethal baritone.

The two beings retreated several more steps before responding. "Warrior, we understand your loss, but your legends are false. There is no Valhalla. There is no Odin, or Thor. These gods, like the gods of the Egyptians and Greeks before you are deceptions, illusions designed to misguide, misdirect and control your species. We created the gods of Egypt and the gods of Greece. The Roman gods were the fallacies of a government wishing to placate and control a large populace just as our ancestors did so many centuries ago."

"You're lying," Kord shot back. "The gods are real. Valhalla is real!"

"We can prove our claim. If you desire to learn the truth about the real history of your world and the role we played in it, follow us." The two turned and exited the room.

Kord tightened the laces on his boots and adjusted the straps on his armor. He picked up the empty sword scabbard, placed it over his shoulder and followed. The Nordic King trailed the frail escorts through several bright hallways. They exited through a series of transparent doors entering a large courtyard.

Duncan Kord's jaw dropped in awe; stunned eyes spied large structures dwarfing even the mightiest castles of his homeland. Dozens of small beings rushed to and fro, busy with some unknown tasks. The mammoth structures cast shadows upon the landscape. The Nordic chieftain was awestruck.

"Even in my dreams, I have never imagined such things." He marveled at the monolithic structures. "Those towers block out the Sun."

One of the tiny beings touched his arm. "Come. There will be time for this later. Right now you must be convinced what we tell you is truth."

Kord nodded, while he studied and absorbed the fantastic sights and sounds of this strange world he'd been cast into unwillingly. As he made his way along the roadway, something struck him as out of place. Though Kord lived most of his life in the woodlands, he'd been to large cities during his travels. He'd sailed to the southern lands and marveled at the fantastic architecture of other societies and races of men. However, nothing he'd ever seen could compare to the sights he beheld this day. Cities were crowded and bustling with activity. Cities possessed the faint miasma of human waste and garbage that was a trademark the world over. This was the main reason he preferred a life outside the protection of castle walls. This city was different. He could smell the trees, and the light crisp breeze had only the scent of salt air and a hint of ozone. This city had an alarmingly small population when compared to its size. There seemed scarcely enough people to inhabit even one of the massive structures dominating the skyline.

Kord continued to walk in silence, his mind carefully studying and observing every detail of this strange place. He'd seen barely a hundred of the beings like those he followed. The Nordic chief estimated that a city of this size could easily contain thousands.

"Where are the rest of your people?"

The beings didn't answer with words. Instead, they gestured for him to follow them into a large round structure.

Kord accompanied them inside the building. His hand absently touched the empty scabbard on his back. He wished his ancestral blade was safely secured where it had been for several years. The inside of the structure was similar to the room he'd been in earlier. The floors and walls emitted a solid white glow. Several colored lights were embedded in the walls and beneath each colored light was a series of what he guessed were crystals of the clearest ruby quartz. One of his escorts approached a nearby panel and depressed two crystals. The crystals sank into the supporting pedestal absorbed into the glowing structure. After a few short moments the walls in front of them darkened and separated. Behind the walls was a cavernous room easily the size of a coliseum.

"By Odin!" Kord gasped. "This place could easily hold thousands of people."

"Ten thousand," one of his escorts replied as a frail hand glided over a flat panel.

The doorway closed behind them and several banks of colored crystals came to life and began humming. The white glow intensified around the room and the floor beneath his feet became a giant map. This map was unlike any he'd ever seen before. The mountains literally rose up from the floor and he could see details of several land masses and oceans taking shape around him. Kord watched fascinated as the three-dimensional map surrounded him. He recognized his homeland and several other landmasses. Other parts of this map were foreign to him. The major landmasses Kord knew seemed slightly different. The great inland sea separating the two major southern landmasses was missing. Both continents were fused into one massive landmass and an unknown large island, roughly the size of the Saxon Empire, occupied a space where he knew only contained miles of empty ocean.

"This map of yours appears to be flawed." The warrior noted as he walked cautiously through the three-dimensional image.

"What you see now is a representation of how the world was nearly one hundred fifty thousand of your years ago. The extra island you see was our home for several thousand of your years. We evolved and developed independently of your kind. Where your species originated from one breed of primate, we evolved and developed from a demure species inhabiting that island. Our species are cousins, warrior. However, we don't possess the barbaric, aggressive tendencies found in mankind."

Kord raised an eyebrow, not sure how to take the slight he'd just been handed. "What changed the world so drastically?" He marveled at the details of the simulated world.

"Our home was formed from a massive undersea volcano."

"A what?"

"Volcano, a mountain that contains passages deep into the earth where molten rock and geothermal gasses can be released onto the surface of this planet," one of the beings explained. "Within the earth are several layers of rock under extreme pressure, this pressure causes enough heat to melt these rocks into a liquid. The pressure upon this liquid rock forces it up towards the surface though cracks and pores within this planet's crust. Volcanoes are like vents, if you will, that allow this liquid rock to be expelled under great force up to the surface. We call this phenomenon an eruption."

Another being spoke. "The undersea volcano that had been dormant beneath our island began to exhibit signs of life. The increasing thermal and geological stress forced us to evacuate our home and relocate on another remote island far away from humanity. We worked for over fifty years building the city you've just traversed. It was to be a home for all Atlanteans. This was to be a new beginning. The heralding of a new golden age."

"Am I to assume this fire mountain erupted before you migrated your people?" Kord felt a pang of remorse over a large loss of life.

"The eruption was more devastating than any of our ancestors anticipated, hundreds of times more volatile," the slim being closest to Kord answered. "We had just begun moving our people and the other native life forms when the first eruption occurred. The inhabitants of Atlantis were destroyed by toxic gasses, volcanic ash, super-heated steam and finally buried under a massive flow of molten rock."

As the demure being spoke, the representation of the island continent began to change. The land mass became black and charred, then slowly sank into the depths of the ocean creating massive waves that swamped all the larger land masses represented on the lifelike map including the lands that represented his home.

"The major blast came several hours later, creating the worst natural disaster since 'The Great Impact' that eradicated the monstrous creatures that laid claim to this world millions of years ago," one of the Atlanteans continued. "The blast caused major earthquakes all around the nearby larger landmasses. Tidal waves taller than our tallest buildings flooded surrounding landmasses wiping out tribes of primitive men and devastating wildlife. The earthquakes caused a portion of a great mountain range to collapse into the sea. The ocean swept in, destroying once fertile land, burying vast tropical forests under tons of rock, sand and mountain debris. The great inland sea was formed dividing one large landmass into two."

Kord watched, mesmerized, as before his eyes, a large section of the mountains fell into the sea allowing billions of gallons of sea water to come crashing inland with devastating force. With incomprehensible power and destruction, the inland sea was created that separated the tribes of the dark-skinned Egyptian warriors from the remnants of the Roman Empire that Pope Leo the First had successfully saved from being sacked by the savage barbarian warrior, Attila the Hun. Kord continued to stare at the map as the water's onslaught buried millions of fertile acres under a cascade of silt, rock, ocean sand and debris from the collapsed mountain range. He'd never seen anything like the images presented by these strange beings. Silently he wondered what means they were using to create these pictures. After several minutes, the inland sea receded slightly and exposed the now barren lands that would become Egypt, Ethiopia, Babylon, Greece, Rome and Jerusalem. The once lush, fertile inland oasis became an extension of the great ocean, while the borderlands surrounding the new body of water transformed into an endless sea of sand. As the Nordic Warrior continued to watch he spotted the mighty Nile River take shape as well as the other two major waterways of the mid-east; the Tigris and Euphrates rivers, which became the 'Mothers Milk' of the desert region and the hubs of Egyptian and Persian commerce. Kord knew some of the history of the world around him, but not enough to even partially comprehend what was unfolding before him.

After several more seconds, the landmasses resembled the maps he knew.

"We are over here, in this small remote island," two beings said in unison pointing toward a small island off the southwestern coast of Africa.

Kord studied the tiny island, barely a spec compared to the great land that sank into the sea. The Nordic king wondered how an entire population could possibly migrate such a great distance, let alone attempt to move native wildlife as well.

"Atlantis," he said with a heavy sigh. "I have heard stories; myths of such a place from travelers and traders from the Southlands. But how does all of this," he gestured toward the large display, "give credence to your claim that Odin and Valhalla are merely myths?"

"What this recreation doesn't show, Warrior, was the cause of all this devastation. We were responsible for the devastation and eradication of hundreds of thousands of humans across several landmasses," one of the slender beings confessed shamefaced.

"By Odin," Kord murmured in awe. "Not even Thor's mighty hammer could wield such devastation as you've shown me this day."

"I wish it were different, human, but truth is truth. Our empire was vast and energy-hungry when we began to tap the vast stores of geothermal power from beneath our island continent. We constructed massive underground power stations to harness the very power of the Earth itself. For centuries we successfully harnessed energy from the depths of the earth. As our cities grew and expanded, we dug deeper into the earth and expanded our power-generating facilities. Many of our scientists warned us that we were weakening the mantle and crust of the Earth beneath our home and risked causing a major eruption. We ignored those warnings until it was too late," one of the beings confessed.

"We assumed that our technology would be able to solve this dilemma before the geological structure of our home became too unstable," the second being continued. "We were wrong. The calamity came earlier and with more devastation than we ever thought possible. Our island nation collapsed under its own weight as a result of our continuous tunneling and construction below the surface. We'd barely migrated one tenth of our population when the first eruption occurred. After that, there was no time to do anything but hope that some of our population managed to escape."

"Did they?" Kord knelt down and passed his hand through a three-dimensional mountain range.

"Two vessels," the slender being nearest him whispered. "Two vessels out of a fleet of fifty."

"And only one of those ships contained the general population of Atlantis. The other vessel contained wildlife to be transplanted and supplies and parts for the maintenance and sustenance of our new city," the second being added.

The Nordic warrior stood and walked away from the impressive map. He felt a great pity for the frail beings. Still, he didn't see how their plight had anything to do with his people, his death or his gods. There was so much to take in and digest. He should be dead, but they managed to reunite his flesh and his spirit. Until this day he'd have sworn that was a feat only the gods could perform. Yet they claimed not to be gods. "I still await your explanation." He grew impatient.

The two beings stared at each other exchanging a dubious look between them. "After the calamity befell all the lands from the great flood, we began to study the effects of the cataclysm we'd created. We destroyed thousands of fledgling human communities bringing the human population to the level of near extinction. Humanity was still barbaric and savage, barely able to comprehend the simplest of tasks. The species of man that was most devastated by the great flood, ironically, was not the species that gave birth to humans, but another type of primitive man. This other type of man had been the dominant species throughout the lands that you know as Egypt, Rome, and Persia. They dominated the fertile delta that is now the inland sea. Your species, though more intelligent, didn't possess the physical strength or endurance that this hardier offshoot of humanity possessed. Had the great calamity not occurred, your species of man would have eventually become extinct. A stronger more aggressive breed of Homo sapiens would have evolved and eventually dominated the planet."

The second being picked up on the story after a brief pause. "We observed your species for several thousand of your years hoping that your race would prosper. Sadly, it did not. Despite your higher intellect, you still seemed determined to exterminate yourselves through petty conflicts. Your race seemed more interested in squabbling amongst themselves than surviving. We decided to intervene, guide your race and help advance it along, hoping that you'd grow civilized and peaceful. We assisted the human evolution process by manipulating the genetics of several members of your species from different geographical locations on this world."

"In essence you've been interfering with our civilizations," Kord interrupted bluntly. "You said you've been manipulating," he paused struggling with the alien word 'Genetics.' "What exactly does that mean and how does it give just cause to your claims about the Gods?" He grew annoyed with this unwelcome history lesson.

The two slender beings stared at each other with visible frustration. "In simpler terms, warrior, we made several of your species smarter – smart enough to assume positions of leadership and authority within their established populations. We, in fact, set ourselves up as gods and worked through these enhanced beings to artificially accelerate the development of your species before men wiped each other off the face of the Earth leaving the cockroaches to inherit this world. Together, the survivors of Atlantis and these altered humans guided your species from fighting with sticks and stones to creating great empires such as Babylon, Egypt, Greece, the Mayans and several Asian dynasties."

Kord was stunned. He'd heard stories of great beings throughout history, powerful leaders that somehow seemed more than human. His own father had captivated him with tales of great Nordic leaders of old, deemed great wise men in possession of untold secrets. Kord knew that, according to the legends of his own people, these leaders were the favored of the gods, often carrying their edicts and judgments. These beings offered a possible explanation for the legends of his own past.

"You took men from my homeland and somehow made them smarter." He understood the titanic implications of what these beings were saying. "And you posed as our gods in order to frighten us into doing your bidding."

"No. Not *our* bidding, but preventing you from slaughtering each other to the point where your species would no longer exist," one of the beings responded. "We had no desire to rule over your kind."

One of the beings motioned toward a device and a three-dimensional image of Odin appeared to materialize from nothingness. As Odin spoke, the room reverberated with the sheer power of his words. The image then shifted to Thor, Kord's preferred god. Thor carried mighty Mjölner, the mystical hammer of power. As the image of Thor spoke, lightning and thunder annunciated every sentence. The next image was Loki, Thor's trickster brother, even the dark court jester of the gods was exactly as legend described. Duncan Kord, Nordic prince, king and warrior of the great northern horde knew they were truthful. If there were no gods, there was no Valhalla. His life had been spent worshiping and paying homage to false idols and a belief that his great mortal deeds would be rewarded in the afterlife.

A wave of grief and agony washed over him. "Enough!" he pleaded. "Better you left me for dead on the field of battle than do this to me." Kord looked up, tears in his eyes. "What you've done is far worse than kill me. You've taken my life, my very existence and made it meaningless and trivial, you've created a façade for all of us."

"We gave your species life!" both beings argued in unison. "If not for us humanity would have died ten thousand years ago or more."

The Nordic man rose, his face now set in stone. "If not for you, demon, there would have been no great disaster, no great flood and the world would have evolved without your interference. For all your magic and god-like powers you are imperfect. You've destroyed yourselves and the rightful future of this world along with you." Kord's tone mimicked the Thunder God.

Silence rang throughout the atrium. The two beings considered his accusations. The supposedly barbaric human stated an undeniable truth.

"What kind of justice is there for murder on such a large scale?" His voice was no longer tainted with anger, only a soft tone of longing and regret over a life lived in homage to phony beliefs and traditions. "What kind of justice can be imparted to a race of wizards that have the power to manufacture castles that touch the clouds or create images from the very air and alter the very essence and fabric of a man?"

One of the frail beings stepped towards Kord and placed a thin hand on his large forearm. "There can be no justice for the things we've done, Duncan Kord. There can be no excuses made for the arrogance of our species and our foolish pride in our self-perceived infallibility. There is a saying in our culture, 'Those that climb the highest have the furthest to fall.' We have fallen from great heights. Our homeland is destroyed, our civilization a fraction of what it once was and the bulk of our people are dead. We've tried to make amends by furthering your species along the technological scale, hoping you could avoid the violence and bloodshed that besets all developing cultures, including our own." The being sighed. "We failed."

"Those we elevated worked for peace and prosperity initially but in the end were corrupted by the aphrodisiacs of wealth and power. Despite all of our intellectual gifts, our chosen were still susceptible to human greed and avarice. One of our most promising humans and biggest failures, Ramses, appointed himself pharaoh over all of Egypt and created a vast empire through conquest. He used our advanced technology to build vast monuments to false gods, to himself and his descendants. Those conquered races were used as slave labor in service to Pharaoh in order to build his temples, statues and eventually a great monolithic pyramid. Our technology allowed them to move massive stones over great distances and raise these large blocks hundreds of feet in the air with ease and precision. Decadence and arrogance led to the fall of Egypt only to be replaced by an even more decadent people: the Greeks." The second being added sadly.

"We had hoped the Greeks would bring about a better age than their predecessors, an age of advanced learning, architecture and culture. Again, it started off as a golden age and we manufactured powerful deities in order to bring a sense of order and law into the populace. We wanted to ward off corruption and arrogance. To counter the gods, those we had so foolishly enhanced created several breeds of horrors to

terrorize the populace and control them. We made a great hero
– a man the Greeks called Hercules, to rid Greece of these
horrors and to perform great deeds and inspire those around
him. In the end, we were working against those we created,
just as before. Greece was following the same path as Egypt
only on a much larger scale. The Greeks we advanced managed
to kill Hercules, like Achilles before him and end the era of
heroes we'd tried to establish. Greek government became
corrupt and more interested in recreational pleasures of the
flesh than affairs of state. In the end, another civilization rose
up, one in which we had no influence or part in creating. That
civilization eventually conquered all and is even now an
influence in your current history."

Kord looked over at them. "Rome," he mumbled struggling
to grasp the story he'd been told.

"Rome," both beings said in unison.

"But not even Rome was eternal, from what little I know of
her history. That empire is long past its greatness," Kord
commented.

"Indeed, the Arabic Muslim population expanded into
Egypt, Mesopotamia and even what remained of the once
mighty Persian Empire. With the words of their prophet
Mohamed to guide them, they spread forth and conquered and
are still conquering to this day," one of the Atlanteans
remarked.

Kord spun toward the frail being who just spoke. "What are
you called? You know my name, my titles and most everything
about me, I'm no longer comfortable conversing with nameless
entities. You aren't demons and you're not gods or demigods.
What do you call yourselves?"

The thinner of the two beings took a step forward, "I am
Saulle, last surviving historian of Atlantis."

"I am Terrel, a cleric and healer. I'm responsible for giving
you back your life, Duncan Kord, Nordic King and Warrior,"
the second whispered. "We and those with us on this tiny
island nation are all that is left of the once-mighty kingdom of
Atlantis."

Kord's head was spinning. It was almost too much for his
mind to comprehend, everything was happening too fast. He
needed time to adjust, accept the loss of his life – his loved ones

and his home – as well as to understand the fantastic tale he'd just been told.

"I cannot imagine what you're feeling or thinking, Duncan Kord." Terrel's voice was a soft, comforting whisper. "We will escort you to quarters where you can rest and consider all that you've seen and heard. We will provide you with sustenance and refreshment if you wish."

Kord did feel tired, but not the kind of fatigue derived from vigorous physical exertion. This was the kind of tired brought about by mental stress and frustration, the kind of stress he'd faced as a leader of his people during times of war and famine.

"I would be grateful for both." Kord followed the two slender beings from the room.

The Nordic leader walked silently through the magnificent city. He didn't pause to marvel at the awe-inspiring structures. His mind was embroiled in a struggle to keep his sanity. Terrel gestured toward a doorway, then entered and continued through a maze of halls. Kord spotted several doors and silently wondered who or what else was living here. Terrel stopped at one door and waved his frail hand over a glowing blue jewel. The doorway slid open and Terrel motioned Kord into the room. The stunned warrior entered cautiously and studied the new surroundings. The room looked comfortable and he sat on an overstuffed chair.

"There is food and water on that table." Terrel pointed toward a multitude of fruits and other foodstuffs.

"Thank you," Kord muttered, not bothering to look up at the tiny Atlantean.

Terrel exited and looked over at Saulle as the door closed, "Do you think he will accept the transition or kill himself as so many others have before him?"

"It is difficult to say," Saulle replied as the two moved away from the doorway and walked down the long corridor lined with doors. "The barbarian has surprised me. He is far more intelligent than I assumed and more capable of adapting than most of the others. Of the six others we took, only the man he was battling and one other are still alive. The other three chose to end their lives rather than accept what we've offered."

"That's twenty dead by suicide, five killed during transition and three successes since we've begun this endeavor." Terrel paused momentarily to study a doorway with flashing red crystal in front of it. He waived his hand over the crystal. "Now there are only the two Nordic warriors left, Kord and Sagahr, from this harvest, plus the other warrior we took earlier. We have altered the Mongol, and the dragons will complete the genetic modifications on Duncan Kord, if he allows it."

"It will have to be enough," Saulle replied as they continued down the hallway and left the building. He looked back at the glowing crystal. "I'll have that room cleansed once the body is removed."

Kord was halfway through the large bowl of fruit before his hunger pangs subsided. However different and strange these beings were, they had a human palette. The Nordic warrior studied the strange dark cubes on the plate next to the fruit. Their scent was inviting and he cautiously picked one up and placed it under his nose. The aroma was pleasant and reminded him of a well-seasoned chunk of beef. He bit into the cube and was pleasantly surprised by its bold flavor and texture. He ate several more of the cubes savoring the delicate yet robust flavor.

He stood, pacing back and forth, contemplating every scrap of information they'd offered and everything he'd observed while outside the large complex. The smell of salt in the air was indeed strong giving credence to their claims of being on an island. The exotic fruits he'd just consumed also seemed to verify that assumption. As far as what he'd witnessed in the large room, he had no plausible explanation. They had the ability to manufacture pictures and images of people or gods from the very air. These beings even seemed to have the power over life and death. His very existence was proof enough of that. The Nordic king wasn't much of a believer in magic but what he'd witnessed defied any rational explanation or reason. They were clearly more advanced in the areas of science and medicine. He wondered how a modern sword would appear to his ancestors that fought with sticks and stones. A steel sword would be a deep mystery, almost magical in its killing ability. He knew his analogy was weak, but it gave him a basis to build some rational explanations for what was occurring and that was a beginning.

Kord walked over to the door and waived his hand in front of the glowing blue crystal as he'd seen the Atlanteans do countless times. The crystal flickered briefly but nothing happened. He attempted to open the door but found it locked. He gently pushed against the barrier but found it firm and solid. The Nordic man impulsively smashed his powerful fists against the doorway, not out of rage or anger, but to get a true measure of the door's strength. The power of his blows reverberated throughout the metal door and frame, but the barrier remained solid. Kord knew his blows would have pulverized any wooden doorway.

"Locked in like some errant child. I am a prisoner after all." He turned from the door. Kord sat on the edge of a comfortable cushion and ran his calloused hands across the sides of his nose and up, across each heavy blond eyebrow. His mind reeled at the impossibility of the events of the past hours. He glanced back over at the locked door and wondered why the Atlanteans felt the need to cage him like some wild animal. Perhaps that's how they viewed him. After all, they had called him a barbarian – and compared to them, he was.

The room took on a surreal quality and the Nordic king felt light headed. The feeling was similar to being drunk; only his thoughts and perceptions were still acute. He knew the food had been tainted. They had poisoned him. His body felt heavy as if he was encased in his heaviest battle armor.

"I'm a man not an animal," he mumbled as he fell backwards on the cushion, unconscious.

The Nordic king awoke and rose unsteadily. He flexed the muscles in his limbs in an effort to increase his circulation and force his body into an alert state. He noted that at some point during his sleep, a fresh bowl of fruit and what appeared to be bread had been delivered along with a pitcher full of amber colored liquid. The strange food cubes he'd consumed earlier were no longer present.

"Fool!" he cursed himself. "You should know better than to eat strange foods."

Kord carefully inspected his body for any signs of tampering. As far as he could tell the Atlanteans had done nothing to him during his forced sleep. He approached the door and tried to open it by waving his hand in front of the crystal, again nothing.

"Still caged." He took the next few minutes and explored his quarters. There was a smaller room that adjoined the larger chamber and, as he entered it, a panel lit up to illuminate the space. Kord wasn't sure of the function of this room but carefully inspected every inch of the small area. He saw two large colored crystals embedded in the far wall above a tiny recessed metallic tub. Kord waved his hand in front of the blue-colored crystal and a slender spigot grew out of the wall and deposited a small stream of water that flowed into the basin and disappeared through a hole in the bottom. Kord cautiously placed his index finger in the stream and felt the familiar sensation of cool water. The warrior cupped his hands and splashed his face with several refreshing handfuls of the liquid. After several seconds, the stream stopped and the spigot vanished inside the wall again. Kord raised an eyebrow clearly impressed. Out of curiosity, he tapped the red crystal and the spigot returned. An identical stream of water flowed but Kord could see steam rising from the water column. He touched the stream and it was hot to the touch but not unbearable. After several seconds the spigot, like before, vanished inside the wall. Kord placed his hand against the wall where the spigot had been and it appeared to be solid.

"How?" He rubbed his finger across the wall.

His observations were interrupted by a series of chimes coming from the other room. Kord walked quickly toward the source of the noise. A small light was blinking over the locked door.

"May we enter?" a voice outside asked.

"Enter," Kord replied.

The once locked door slid open and Terrel and Saulle stepped inside, "We trust you are well rested," the beings said in unison.

"How could I not be," Kord replied, bitter. "Your food was laced with some kind of sleep-inducing poison.

The two slender Atlanteans appeared surprised to have been discovered, "You misunderstand our motive, Duncan Kord. The food cubes contained a mild sedative that helps the imbiber relax. We have no intention of poisoning you; only seeing that you get rest after your ordeal."

"I am well rested," Kord answered, "but curious as to why I'm locked inside like some errant child."

"You're locked in for your own protection. You have no familiarity with our technology or the topography of our city," Saulle explained.

"Though our island is not extensive there are still dangers here that you are not prepared to endure." Terrel added.

"I have faced many dangers in my life, and have been well able to care for and defend not only myself but my people as well." Kord shook his head. "This island of yours seems tame and tranquil compared to my own homeland."

"Believe us when we tell you, Nordic warrior, there are dangers here that even a man as formidable as yourself would be unable to comprehend or cope with."

Kord had no choice but to accept what they said. Whether they felt he was a prisoner or guest, his freedom was limited and his purpose for being reborn was, as of yet, unknown. "I accept your word." He deliberately walked toward the open door. If the Atlanteans attempted to detain him, Kord knew there were other reasons for keeping him penned. Saulle and Terrel parted and allowed Kord to enter the hallway. The two slender beings followed behind in silence. Kord navigated the maze of corridors until he came to the device that had carried them to this floor of the building. Kord glanced back at the two beings.

"I cannot operate the controls."

Terrel silently walked over and waived his hand over the crystal panel and the lift doors parted. Kord stepped in and the two beings followed. After a quick descent, the lift doors opened again and deposited the three in the building's main floor. Kord stepped out and made his way outside. He looked up at the sun and determined it was midmorning. He'd slept for several hours beyond his norm. As he walked, the two Atlanteans struggled to keep up with his quick pace.

"Where are you going?" Terrel asked as Kord moved even faster.

"Away from the city, perhaps to the coastline or deeper into the woodlands," Kord replied. "I've never been comfortable in cities. This one, fantastic as it is, is no exception."

Kord continued toward the outskirts of the city, the tiny Atlanteans following close behind. The claustrophobic confines of streets and buildings – even the modest huts and two-story dwellings of his kingdom – made him feel uncomfortable. He took a quick bearing and headed toward the coast.

"Where are you going?" They asked again in unison.

"To the sea," Kord shouted over his shoulder. "It's been many days since I was able to enjoy the sounds of the ocean. All that I have is gone; all that I was is no more. I wish to be alone with my thoughts and grieve for my losses." He pointed toward them. "Perhaps your kind is beyond personal attachments, but I am not. I've lost my queen and I've lost my brother and son. I've lost my kingdom and I should have lost my life. Better you had left me to die with dignity amongst my kinsmen on the field of battle." The Viking warrior vanished into the woods. Terrel and Saulle watched impassively as the forest swallowed him and they stared at each other.

"He grieves for his past. None of the others did so," Terrel observed.

"He was a leader of many," Saulle replied. "Sadly, he has lost much. The fact that he grieves at all proves he has compassion along with wisdom. Notice how, unlike the others, he spoke of his bond mate and kin. There has been no mention of the loss of personal wealth or status despite his position as ruler. I think our neighbors were right about this particular human."

"Shall we follow him?" Terrel gestured toward the point where Kord vanished into the jungle.

"No," Saulle answered, "Let him be alone with his grief, for now."

"What about the creatures that roam the jungle, coastlines, and the skies?"

"We cannot protect him. We cannot interfere. The barbarian is strong and skilled. He will have to rely on those talents if he wishes to leave the protection our city offers. We did warn him and can do no more, I will, however, inform our allies of his whereabouts. They can protect him if necessary"

Both beings turned and headed back toward their towering city leaving Duncan Kord alone to deal with his grief and to face the unknowns of the Atlantean jungle.

Kord covered nearly six miles of wooded terrain. Sharp ears detected the sound of surf coming from the west. The northern king was unaccustomed to the humidity and heat but ignored the discomforts of the tropical climate as best he could. He removed his heavy garments and armor, securing them behind a small bush for later retrieval and proceeded, shirtless, traveling only in his heavy boots and a makeshift loincloth of deer skin. He marveled at the fantastic array of colorful birds and small reptiles that took refuge on the Atlantean island. He'd heard stories from free traders about lands such as these but never imagined he'd have the opportunity to see such a rich array of teeming life in one small area. Unlike his rugged homeland, where the cool bite of winter was ever-present and game could be scattered over several square miles, this place contained evidence of a dense population of animals. He paused, kneeling down beside a well-used deer trail. Curious, he followed the path for several yards traveling deeper into the jungle. Kord spotted a fresh pile of droppings and examined them.

"Similar to a deer, but what would they feed upon here?" he crumbled a pellet between his fingertips. The texture was different than what he was familiar with and he knew that indeed the herbivores here had a radically different diet than the rough grasses and ferns found in his homeland. He tossed the pellet away, wiped his hand on a nearby leaf and continued to follow the trail deeper into the jungle. Kord was so engrossed in his diversion, he ignored the warning his senses had been providing him for several minutes. He felt that familiar tingle at the base of his neck and he knew he was being watched. He spun around quickly expecting to see the two frail Atlanteans but all he saw was the path he'd been following and more thick vegetation. Kord didn't accept that. He remembered how the two beings had been invisible to his eyes earlier, yet he knew they'd been there. The battle-hardened warrior was seasoned enough to know never to rely on one sense. What his eyes didn't see, his sharp ears heard; movement from above concealed by the dense leaf canopy. Kord took cover behind a thick tree trunk. His eyes scanned the immediate area for some kind of weapon. He silently cursed the Atlanteans for depriving him of his sword, whatever the reason. As Kord hid behind the tree his nose detected the fetid stench of death. He glanced behind him and spied the half-eaten carcass of a deer-like creature; only this animal was easily twice the size of any deer he'd ever seen. From what he could see, the great beast had been literally torn apart.

"By Odin, what manner of creature could kill something so large?" Kord knew the kill was fresh, barely several hours old. Whatever manner of beast had made the kill would no doubt return to continue feeding. The Nordic warrior had to get away from this area quickly. He cautiously moved forward, never taking his eyes off the dense canopy of leaves and vines. As he moved, he could hear something in the trees pacing him. The crack of displaced air disturbed the silence. Whatever was up there had wings. Kord fought the basic human instinct to run. Running now would alert whatever creature was up there that he was frightened. Panicked motion would cause the creature to instinctively attack. He ducked under overhangs and hugged tree trunks, never straying onto the open game trail. If he exposed himself for even a moment, he'd be vulnerable. Kord forced his way through the dense growth heading back towards the coastline.

He heard the waves breaking against the beach and gave silent thanks his actions baffled his pursuer. The blond man crouched behind a large boulder listening for the telltale noises in the treetops before leaving the protective cover. The jungle was quiet aside from several birds and a multitude of annoying insects. All the while, beads of sweat continued to pour off Kord's body, making him more impatient and more uncomfortable. After ten minutes, he was convinced whatever was following him had moved on, perhaps back toward the fresh kill. Kord crept from his place of concealment and headed down the sandy beach toward the inviting ocean. When he was no more than twenty feet from the water's edge he heard the crack of large wings. His instincts shrieked danger and the warrior dove and somersaulted to his right side. As he moved, Kord felt a burning pain across his back and shoulders.

Kord quickly gathered himself and crouched in a battle-ready position. The thing that attacked him had flown over the shallows, banking around for another crack at him. Kord frantically looked for some kind of weapon, anything that might provide an aid in protecting his life. All he saw was an endless ribbon of sand. He had to stand and fight. If he turned and ran toward the jungle, the flying creature would pick him off easily as he fled. As the thing completed its turn, it let out a cackle sending a chill through him. The beast looked like a cross between a large lizard and a bat. Kord noted that this flying beast had an overly large head filled with long jagged teeth and though, like a bird, it had no arms, its legs were long and extremely muscular. As the thing rushed toward him, it swept its claws forward like a gigantic hawk would as it approached a rabbit or rodent. Kord counted four seconds, timing the thing's approach and guessing how quickly it could react once he started moving again. He forced himself to remain alert, yet motionless, despite the creature bearing down on him. As he reached the fourth second, his powerful leg muscles flexed propelling away from the oncoming horror. Kord felt the whistle of the wind as the beast raced by the spot he'd been only a heartbeat earlier. The creature banked sharply, barely avoiding the trees as it turned for another attack.

Kord turned and fled into the ocean, hoping to hide himself in the cool depths of the water. The Nordic king struggled to control his fear, but felt the raw emotion rising unchecked as he plunged deeper into the sea. He instinctively knew that the creature was bearing down on him and would strike again within seconds. Through his rising fear, his instincts told him to dive. He plunged down into the salty water ignoring the burning sensation caused by the brine contacting his torn flesh. The water above him exploded violently as razor sharp talons raked the shallows looking for their prey. He felt a sharp pain in his right calf and knew the beast had cut deeply into his leg. Kord kept swimming, propelling his body deeper and deeper into the sea. He glanced up quickly as several bubbles escaped his lungs and gently floated to the surface. He gauged his depth around ten to twelve feet. He saw the dark mass of his nemesis circling overhead waiting for him to surface. This creature was smart. Somehow it knew he'd have to come up for air. At that time Kord would be vulnerable to attack.

Kord's lungs were burning, begging for fresh oxygen and his back and calf stung from exposure to the salt water. He swam several yards away from the circling monster and approached the surface. Before he could gather a life-giving breath, the creature was upon him. Razor sharp claws clamped down upon his heavy shoulders and grabbed him like a vice. He fought bravely but was plucked from the water like an eagle taking a salmon from a lake. He gazed down at the ocean and saw the visible blood trail that the beast had used to track his submerged movements. Desperation and fear drove him into action. He grabbed the scaly legs of his captor and squeezed them in grips of iron. Kord's powerful forearms were shaking from the force of his exertion. His fingers dug into the thin, scaly flesh and crushed fragile tendons and ligaments. The beast roared in pain and surprise, unaccustomed to prey that fought back. The creature reluctantly let go of its captive, but Kord refused to give up his grip, he guessed he was fifty feet in the air and he knew a fall from this height into the shallow waters would kill him. He squeezed his forearms with all his might and was rewarded with the sound of cracking bone and sinew. The claws that had held him so firmly were now nothing more than useless appendages. The great beast cried out in shrill agony and its high-pitched shriek was no longer the triumphant call of an apex predator but was the sound of an animal in distress.

The numbing pain caused the creature to lose valuable altitude and it began to plummet into the shallows. The creature sensed the danger and began frantically beating its massive leathery wings in an effort to climb higher into the sky. Kord knew it was now or never. He let go of the scaly legs and fell into the shallows. He curled himself into a tight ball as he impacted the ocean surface. He hit the ocean floor with bone jarring force, but the water cushioned enough of the impact to keep the warrior from serious injury. Kord slowly rose to the surface and took a much-needed deep breath. The creature he'd battled landed on shore and was struggling to walk on ruined claws. It flopped around wildly in an effort to stand on legs of shattered bone and crushed tissue. Kord cautiously emerged from the ocean careful to keep a safe distance between himself and the wounded predator. The beast spotted its prey on the beach and awkwardly moved toward him. Wings and legs worked together in a bizarre fashion to propel it forward. With two great beats, the creature was airborne again.

"By the gods, this ends now!" Kord shouted, preparing to confront the incoming monstrosity. The Nordic warrior let go of his fear as frustration. Anger boiled through his fatigued body. Hate and desperation provided the energy to continue the fight for his life. The creature glided in for the kill. Its legs extended forward in an effort to pluck from the ground. Kord could see that the razor-sharp talons hung limp and useless at the end of each appendage. There was no fear and the Nordic king held his ground and shouted a defiant battle cry at the top of his lungs. The creature made its pass and flailed awkwardly at him with shattered claws. Instead of avoiding the attack, Kord charged the incoming terror and the two combatants collided. The impact caused both man and beast to topple in a pile upon the damp sand. The beast struggled, flapping its large wings while snapping its massive jaws at Kord's head and torso. Face to face, Kord finally got a measure of this terror. It was several feet taller than he stood, and its skin, though scaly, wasn't rough or textured like he'd expected. Kord ducked under the snapping maw and unleashed a series of powerful blows into the thing's midsection. The creature buckled slightly and fell backward. The beast planted itself firmly on the sand using its feet like anchors. It was changing strategy to compensate for its handicap.

It dawned on Kord that this was no mere mindless monster. It had the ability to think, learn and reason. He knew his reserves were failing rapidly and if he didn't find a way to kill this creature, he'd wind up like the carcass he stumbled upon earlier. Kord knelt down, feigning weakness. As he did, he scooped up a large handful of sand. The creature took the opportunity to hop in with a short flap of its wings. It landed awkwardly and adjusted its stance quickly. During that brief pause, Kord sprang up and threw the handful of sand directly into the beast's eyes. A large cloud of sand covered the creature's head and it shrilled in surprise. It stumbled backward and fell, landing on its back. Having no hands to clear its eye sockets, the beast flailed back and forth wildly in an attempt to clear the debris from its sensitive eyeballs. Kord leapt on top of the larger creature and grabbed its head in both hands. Before the beast's large hind legs could reach up and tear into him, the Nordic warrior snapped the large head forcefully in a counterclockwise direction and then quickly snapped it clockwise. Kord was rewarded with the sound of bone shearing and breaking. The beast gave out one last high-pitched squeal before it died. Kord was silent for several heartbeats as he studied the beast. Then he looked up to the heavens and shouted a victory cry.

As the echoes of his scream faded, the exhausted warrior detected more activity within the jungle treetops. To his horror several more of the creatures took to the air in response to the slain beast's final call.

"It appears I am to die after all."

The Nordic chieftain had nothing left. A wave of dizziness overtook him. He'd lost far too much blood. One of the things spotted him and called to the others. They closed for the kill. Kord stumbled away from the beast he'd slain and stood out in the open.

"I am Duncan Kord, Warrior Chieftain of the northern tribe!" He shouted at the top of his lungs. "Which of you foul beasts are next to taste my wrath?" Kord fell to his knees as his wounded leg buckled. He continued to stare at the oncoming creatures as they roared in anticipation of an easy kill. "Odin, may I die well." Kord watched with an unusual detachment as the largest of the beasts broke ranks and swooped down toward him. Its mouth opened revealing hundreds of sharp teeth that would cut him to pieces with one snap of its jaws. The warrior waited, welcoming the chance to be with his wife and brother, wherever they may be in the afterlife. Kord struggled to stay conscious as the beast swept along the coast preparing to kill him. Before the creature could reach the battered warrior, it was consumed in a stream of bright green fire. The stream of flame vaporized it, then struck the ground fusing the nearby sand into a molten pool of glass. A mammoth shadow passed over Kord's head causing him to look up with wonder.

A gigantic winged reptile, easily three times larger than the creature he'd slain, flew toward the remaining beasts at breathtaking speed. Another volley of greenish fire engulfed two more of the smaller things. The creatures were screeching in panic and diving back into the cover of the jungle canopy. Kord watched fascinated as the great beast fired another green salvo into the treetops. Everything the fire touched was either burnt or vaporized on contact. Kord fought to stay conscious, ignoring the spasms of his overworked body. With great effort he stood watching his winged savior cleanse the jungle. The great reptile gracefully banked back toward the ocean. Kord watched transfixed as the massive creature touched down barely ten feet away from him. He gazed in awe at the head that easily towered twenty feet over his.

The reptile's eyes glowed with the same green fire that dispatched the smaller devils. But there was something in those eyes – a deep intelligence, a presence of thought and intellect – that reverberated throughout the entire creature's being. Kord instinctively knew that standing before him was an intelligence and wisdom surpassing his own.

"I owe you my life." Kord bowed his head in thanks and respect to his savior. The beast tilted itself over, balancing perfectly on muscular hind legs, lowering its regal head so it was eye-level with the stunned human. Unlike the smaller beasts, this elegant giant had arms as well as wings. Its arms were somewhat shorter than its powerful hindquarters but were thick with muscle, tendon and bone. Kord's savior dropped to all fours and took a step closer to the human. Kord didn't retreat; he stood absolutely still, never taking his eyes off the twin burning green embers that seemed to study him closely. The beast's head came within inches of Kord's face, and the warrior could clearly hear the loud trip-hammer beating of his heart. The battle-weary human could hear the great intakes of air as the giant drew breath and exhaled. The gale force tossed his long hair back and made him retreat a step.

"Can you understand me?" Kord struggled to keep his head held high.

The creature said nothing but continued to study him. The adrenaline from the battle had worn off and the blood loss fatigued already weakened muscles. Blue sparkles danced in front of his eyes as a sheet of black replaced his peripheral vision. Kord knew within seconds he'd be unconscious and dead shortly after. The battered warrior tried to speak one more time but collapsed in a heap on the sand. The great beast stood guard over the fallen human. It stood on its hind legs and looked up toward the sky and roared a warning call that echoed throughout the entire jungle. The sound faded into an eerie silence. The jungle sounds ceased and only the crackling of flames, still burning from the creature's green fire, could be heard in the distance. The creature's majestic head scanned the beach and peered into the jungle as if awaiting a challenge to its self-proclaimed dominance. In the distance, a silver disk skimmed over the treetops. The creature unfurled its huge wings and was airborne with one powerful beat. The air crackled like thunder as each wing beat propelled the creature away at fantastic speed.

Kord awoke back in the quarters he'd left prior to venturing out into the jungle. For several moments he thought the creatures were figments of his tortured mind, the products of a dream world, for only in such a place could such creatures dwell. As he rose from the bed, a searing wave of pain shot through his back, and his right calf throbbed in subtle agony. As he swung his legs over the side of the bed, he noticed a long, purple scar starting at the back of his knee and ending just above his heel. He paused, momentarily studying the battered flesh and nodded his head in approval. To a warrior king this was a noble wound, earned from honorable combat. As he stood, his leg protested. A searing hot pain burned his back.

"By Odin!" He winced in discomfort. "It was no dream." Kord limped to the back room and waived his hand in front of the red crystal as he'd done before. The slender spigot slid through the wall, immediately followed by a stream of hot water. He splashed several handfuls of water on his face and arms. He could still smell the salty brine of the ocean in his hair and on his body. Somehow, they'd managed to find him before those other creatures could make a meal of him. He wondered if any had survived the inferno. Kord thought about the large beast that saved him from certain death. As a warrior and king, he'd traveled to different parts of the world and witnessed many wonders but nothing could compare to the majesty of the large reptile. Kord shuddered as he recalled the twin burning green embers that studied him with an almost casual curiosity.

"That's twice I've cheated death. The third time will be my undoing." Kord noticed a large flat reflective surface on the far wall. He painfully made his way over to it and turned so that his back faced the shiny area. When he turned his head, he could see the deep lacerations covering his entire back. Kord noticed that the wounds had scarred over and weren't seeping, as cuts of that nature would be after such a short time. How long had he been sleeping? "Just how much control do these Atlanteans have over me?" He walked back to the main room and flopped heavily upon the large cushion that was his bed. He reached for a piece of fruit from the nearby bowl.

Part of being a good ruler and general was adapting to change and adjusting to unforeseen circumstances. His family was gone, his countrymen were corpses scattered over a battle ground half a world away. So much to adapt to and accept in such a short time. Kord waited for a huge wave of grief to overwhelm him. There was no emotion, just an empty numbness, as if this were all a mead-induced dream. It wasn't a dream. He was here, kept by beings that claimed no kinship with man yet enjoyed directing and controlling the fates of men and their empires. He contemplated escape. Where could he run? The jungles outside the city were wrought with horrors beyond imagining and creatures that had no inherent fear of man. There were no ships heading back to his kingdom. Even if he could hijack a ship, his home was gone, trampled over by the barbarian, Sagahr and his hordes along with the northern neighbors that coveted his land.

A chime disturbed his thoughts. He knew it was Terrel and Saulle. "Enter." He stood to face his hosts.

Terrel and Saulle entered quickly. A long table floated in behind them of its own volition.

"I'm pleased to see you've recovered from your ordeal, Kord," Terrel began. "We thought you perished when we heard the distress call from our neighbor."

"I would have died out there." Kord faced the lean figure. He was somewhat taken aback. These beings knew his large reptilian savior. "A large winged creature saved me from certain doom."

"Takeara said you fought valiantly against the wyvern and deserved rescue." Saulle's voice brimmed with excitement.

"Wyvern," Kord repeated, associating the name with the nine-foot winged demon that nearly killed him. "What manner of creature is this Takeara you speak of?"

Takeara is the king of a race of beings called dragons. Dragons predate mankind and even Atlanteans by several thousand decades. They've inhabited this planet for millions of years, even surviving the great calamity that ended the age of thunder beasts when the great rock fell from the sky and covered the Earth in ash and toxin. The dragon ancestors flew to the island we called Atlantis and found sanctuary in the warmth and shelter of the numerous volcanic caverns," Saulle explained.

Kord sensed the growing excitement in the tiny being's voice. For the first time, they seemed anxious and agitated. Kord found their normal excessive calm disturbing. "You seem on edge," the warrior commented hoping his hosts would elaborate.

Terrel stepped forward. "You've earned the respect of a dragon, Duncan Kord. No human in the history of mankind can make such a claim. Very few of our species have such an honor."

"I'm honored such a noble creature finds merit in me, though somewhat puzzled as to why. If it hadn't interfered, I'd be in the stomachs of those things. That creature..." Kord paused as he recalled the overwhelming presence his winged savior commanded, "...nay, that being! That being has an intelligence and bearing far surpassing anything I've ever encountered."

"Very few can detect the intellect of a dragon, Duncan Kord. We wouldn't have thought it possible among humans," Saulle replied with an uncharacteristic lilt of excitement.

Kord's eyes fell upon the floating table. He recognized the shape of the object covered by white linen. "My sword!" He made his way toward the table.

"No!" Terrel shouted, blocking Kord's path. "You cannot handle the blade just yet. Your body isn't fully compatible with the weapon. It will reject you."

Kord stopped his approach. "What do you mean? What have you done to my ancestral blade?"

"We've altered the chemical makeup of the sword's metal and infused it with materials from our laboratory and rare, powerful elements provided us by Takeara. We've added a genetic lock to the blade so that only your unique biological signature will be able to wield the weapon and harness its power."

Kord didn't fully understand Terrel's answer. "If the weapon is bound to me as you say, why should I hesitate to pick it up?"

"Our scientists have altered the base genetic code the sword will respond to – your essence combined with that of a dragon's. That unique combination is the only sequence that can now wield the sword," Saulle answered using the unemotional tone Kord had grown accustomed to hearing.

Uncontrollable anger coursed through the Nordic king's body. He forcefully shoved the frail being aside, yanked off the linen, and exposed his weapon. The blade he saw hardly resembled the weapon he'd wielded all his adult life. The sword's blade was now nearly four feet in length and seemed to shift in color from shades of green to silver to gold depending how the light danced upon the metallic surface. The sword's hilt that had once been wrapped in simple doeskin leather was now intricately bound in some type of braided dark wire mesh and the cross guard had been reforged with intricate engravings upon the eerie metal glowing with an unknown power. Before either Atlantean could react, he hungrily reached out and grasped the sword. The weapon reacted violently and Kord was bathed in jagged arcs of angry, emerald energy. The warrior was flung, stunned, across the length of his room, He slammed into the opposite wall with bone jarring force. He stood weakly and stumbled forward. He looked upon the weapon, reaching for it again. His hand stopped inches from the hilt as he observed more jagged arcs of energy jumping from the sword as it detected his approach.

Kord pulled his hand back. Angry eyes studied the two beings as they observed him in silence. "Is this some kind of warped torture? Why would you do this to me? Have I not lost enough in one lifetime to satisfy you that you seek to punish me further?"

"We have no wish to torture you, Nordic king, but we do have need of your talents and uniqueness," Terrel answered. "We have invested many resources bringing you back from oblivion. We have need of a warrior to unite us with our dragon brothers and lead them in defense of our home."

"The dragons seem more than able to defend themselves, as the wyverns can attest." Kord rubbed his shoulder. The Nordic king was still somewhat shaken by the force his body had endured.

"Agreed," both Atlanteans said in unison, "but they are too few in numbers and the lead male is advanced in years and can no longer sire the next generation."

Kord was annoyed. They were too cryptic. He slammed his fist against a nearby table, shattering it to fragments. "By Odin, be direct with me! Just tell me what plan you have in simple tongue. I'm weary of your evasiveness and mystery. My temper grows short, as does my tolerance for your theatrics!" he growled in a lethal baritone.

The Atlanteans cowered from Kord's wrath. "Accompany us to the dragon caves, Warrior, and we will reveal all to you. You'll understand why you've been brought here and what's expected of you." Terrel's voice echoed his fear. "Will you accompany us there?"

"I will," Kord answered flatly. "And I had better get all the information I seek." Angry knuckles cracked.

Saulle nodded nervously. "All will be revealed to you then, you have our word."

"Lead on." Kord pointed toward the open doorway.

The Secrets of the Dragon Caves
A New Beginning
Dragon's Lair, New Atlantis

Kord and the Atlanteans traveled by hovercraft, gliding over an overgrown path. Terrel landed the vehicle in a small clearing and both Atlanteans made their way into the jungle. Kord disembarked, marveling at the fantastic craft. He followed his hosts into the inhospitable jungle toward the island's mountainous region. The warrior uprooted a small tree and fashioned a makeshift club. He would have preferred his sword, but the accursed beings had worked their sorcery on his blade. A loud rustling in the treetops ended his contemplation. Kord stepped in front of the tiny beings, holding his club above his head, ready for the slightest danger.

"The wyvern will not venture into dragon territory. We have no need to fear them." Terrel gestured toward a group of monkeys leaping from treetop to treetop. "These primates are not a threat. We are a day's travel from any dangerous creatures."

Kord watched the monkeys disappear into the distant tree canopy. He lowered his weapon, feeling foolish. "It never hurts to be prepared," he replied defensively as he walked down the trail. Both Atlanteans grinned and quickly followed.

They traveled three miles through the meandering jungle path, climbing higher and higher into the elevated lands of New Atlantis. Kord spotted several dragons circling overhead. "By the gods! Look at them!" They were riding midday thermals roaring to each other in some sort of communication. Kord and the two Atlanteans approached a huge cavern.

"The home of the dragons," Terrel whispered. Kord looked up at the flying dragons, admiring their grace and elegance. There was something different about these airborne dragons; they seemed much slimmer than the one he'd encountered at the beach.

"Females?" he mumbled.

"I did not hear you." Terrel looked up at the Nordic warrior. The warrior looked back. "I said 'females'? Those in the skies lack the sheer bulk of Takeara. I'm guessing those are females or perhaps younglings."

As they approached the cave entrance, three dragons greeted them. Kord spun his club, raised it in a gesture of respect and then, with dramatic flair, split the weapon over his massive thigh and tossed the broken pieces in front of the three dragons. One of the dragons looked at the large blond warrior and roared in approval. Another spun its head toward the club and unleashed a volley of fire. This fire wasn't the greenish weapon Kord witnessed earlier. It seemed remarkably similar to a natural flame. The club pieces, however, were incinerated to ash. The dragons formed up around the three humanoids escorting them inside the cave.

"Why did you destroy your weapon?" Saulle whispered as they made their way down a long corridor.

"To carry an exposed weapon into what is supposed to be a friend's village is an indication of either aggressive intent or a sign you feel threatened. Neither case applies here. I have no desire to offend our hosts and be part of a dragon barbecue. By destroying the weapon as I did, I demonstrated our confidence in their good faith and proclaimed a decree that we have peaceful intentions. I can only assume that her burning of the club pieces is an acknowledgment of our peaceful gesture," Kord whispered, marveling at the titanic cavern. "I hope."

Kord was quick to note their three escorts were fifteen to twenty felt in length. When down on all fours, they stood slightly taller than he did. Up close, he could see powerful muscles and tendons sheathed beneath what he assumed were iron-hard scales. Each motion these creatures made was precise, every move a ballet of balance and agility. The large, powerful human felt awkward and clumsy as he stumbled upon the gravel path compared to his escorts.

As they walked deeper into the cave, the heat became more oppressive. Kord detected a powerful, musky scent. The Atlanteans seemed unaware of the odor. Kord felt strangely alert and unusually calm. There was something welcoming about this cave. Without even realizing what he was doing, he found himself gently patting the hind flank of one of the great beasts. The she dragon purred in response to his touch. She swung her head around and regarded the Nordic king with a look of genuine affection. "Your home is magnificent!" Kord gently stroked the top of her large head as he continued along the rocky path.

Terrel and Saulle feel back, observing Kord.

"He is already accepted by them." Terrel marveled at the subconscious interaction between man and dragon.

"Takeara said there was one who shared their heart. They've felt his life force since his conception," Saulle replied, equally amazed at how the human easily interacted with the reptilian beings he'd never encountered before. "It appears we have truly found that being. Perhaps now we can be forgiven for destroying our home."

"How many dragons didn't make migration, Saulle? How many were lost in the hatcheries during the great calamity? We have performed a service for our friends, but have not yet earned the right to expect forgiveness or redemption for our brash arrogance."

"Indeed, but perhaps in time."

"Perhaps." Terrel nodded. "But we have committed other crimes against our dragon neighbors that we may never be able to atone. We can only hope the desperation of our plight justifies our action." Terrel paused and the group rounded a corner, "We are almost to the chamber. I confess to being somewhat anxious as to the outcome of our endeavor."

The rocky path ceased and opened into a titanic chamber. The three dragons took to the air and flew to separate perches in the cavern. The heat was extreme and Kord could feel perspiration pour from his body. In the center of the cavern, surrounded by a dozen she dragons, sat the creature that saved Kord's life. It was easy to see the differences between the male and female. Takeara easily towered over the females around him. The musculature of his arms and legs clearly set

balance of their reproductive cycle was thrown into chaos due to the accident that destroyed our continent. Many dragons perished and the cycle that kept their population steady has been ruined. A new bull could father a fresh generation of young and partially reset the cycle of the species, restoring a balance that's been disrupted for millennium." The frail being took a step away from Kord.

The Nordic king laughed, shaking his head. "I think you Atlanteans need a basic lesson in nature. I'm a man. I'm not quite equipped for what you have in mind and I don't think the ladies of this community would welcome whatever advances I made upon them."

"As a man, no," Terrel agreed, "but as a male dragon you would be welcomed into the clan as a king."

"Which goes back to my original remark," Kord grew annoyed, "I am not a dragon, nor will I ever be a dragon. Even a blind man can see the obvious flaw in your plan."

Saulle pointed toward Takeara. "He can correct that. He has the ability to make one man – a man that is possessed with the soul of a dragon – into one of their kind. You'll be both man and dragon, Duncan Kord. You don't realize how unique you really are and for how many centuries we've been searching for you."

Kord's survival instincts triggered. He withdrew several steps from the mammoth reptile and the Atlanteans. "You say you want to make me into a one of them? You'll forgive me if I decline such an offer. I'm in no hurry to forsake my humanity."

Kord turned toward the large opening and became keenly aware of three jills blocking his exit. The Nordic warrior was trapped. He knew, unarmed, he was no match for even a single dragon let alone an entire cave full of them. He turned back toward the Atlanteans and Takeara. "Is this what you had in mind for me all along? Is this why you brought me back to the land of the living?" His voice seethed with anger and defiance. "You'll have to kill me, again, for I'll not submit willingly!" He raised his powerful arms in a protective manner, preparing his body for oblivion.

Takeara slowly approached the defiant human, Kord's eyes narrowed to slits and his muscles tensed, preparing for the inevitable green inferno that would vaporize him into nothingness. The mighty bull dragon dropped on all fours staring directly into Kord's eyes. Kord didn't waiver or break the gaze. As he looked up into the eyes of the mighty beast, he could sense the creature's thoughts and intellect.

You are one of us, Duncan Kord. I knew as I saw you battle the wyvern, you fought with the heart and soul of a dragon. We are bound together, look into yourself and learn what you truly are.

Images of a life totally alien to anything he'd ever seen inundated Kord's mind. He saw a mammoth cave populated with hundreds of dragons all living in harmony and balance. The Nordic king experienced living flight from Takeara's memories, soaring and gliding higher into the morning sky with mighty wings spread open to catch Atlantis's early thermals. He experienced a sense of kinship and camaraderie with the dragons he was seeing in his mind. Each individual had a name and a long family history. There was no greed or malice in these noble creatures. They weren't driven by a desire for riches, fame or power. Petty human concepts were incomprehensible to dragon culture. The sense of pride and love for family the Nordic king experienced through the dragon king was overwhelming. The great bull loved and respected each of his mates and they, in turn, loved him without resentment or jealousy toward each other. In Duncan Kord's mind the dragons were living in the closest thing to a utopian society his limited human mind could comprehend.

Through Takeara, Kord witnessed the demise of Atlantis. He watched in horror as a wall of molten rock engulfed the dragon caves, smothering the hatcheries, cooking the unhatched eggs. The lava flow overwhelmed dozens of dragons. Their iron-hard flesh could withstand extreme temperatures, so they weren't incinerated. Instead, they drowned and burned internally as they involuntarily inhaled the searing magma in place of air. Kord wept openly as he experienced the senseless slaughter of so many noble creatures. He witnessed the dragon migration as the last remnants of the species followed the two surviving Atlantean transports to their new island home.

Kord felt, through the great reptile, the moment of his birth. Somehow the dragons sensed his arrival. They were indeed threaded by a bond of kinship. Kord experienced his comparatively brief life through impulses and tremors of emotion upon Takeara's conscious and subconscious mind. Takeara sensed his battle with Sagahr and his barbarian minions. Somehow the dragon king knew the human would be murdered. It was Takeara that sent the Atlantean vessel to recover him.

You are our last hope Nordic king; you can have eternal life and power beyond the imaginings of any mortal. Your heart and your soul are untainted by the greed and avarice prevalent in your species. Join with us, become a lord of the dragons and take your rightful place as leader of the last dragon clan of Atlantis. Takeara's thoughts whispered inside the Nordic king's mind.

Kord looked within himself and realized everything the Atlanteans told him was truthful; he was linked to these noble creatures. All his life he'd struggled to create a kingdom that was both peaceful and prosperous. Kord realized his ideals were the ideals of the dragon. He was unlike the savage barbarians of the northeast and unlike his own Nordic counterparts. He wasn't interested in conquest or war, or even the wealth inherent within his own kingdom. Everyone in Kord's kingdom prospered and each citizen was valued. It was as ideal a society as could be achieved by Man. A tingling coursed through his spine and spread throughout his body. Goosebumps covered his flesh as he came to grips with everything he'd been told. The dragon's offered him a new beginning, a chance to explore another part of himself, a part buried inside his humanity for the sparse thirty-five years he'd been alive.

He looked over at the two Atlanteans then focused his gaze up at the titanic reptile. "Can what you say really be done? Can you actually make me a dragon as well as a man?"

"We can't. Takeara can. Only a man with the heart and soul of a dragon could survive this particular transformation. That man is you, Nordic king." Terrell replied.

Kord ran his hand through his long hair as he considered the offer before him. He had nothing left in his life. Everything he'd held dear was gone. Perhaps this was his true destiny. The chance to be a part of such a unique community was more than anything he'd ever imagined. This was a chance at life, a new beginning. All he had to do was take it. "I accept."

Terrel nodded toward Takeara. With a deliberate slow motion, the reptile swung its tail forward. From the tip of its tail emerged a needle-like barb. Before Kord could react, the tail shot forward impaling him in the chest. As the Nordic king's body registered the impact, Takeara's tail had already swung back behind the dragon's body. Kord's hand rubbed the point of impact. It didn't hurt like a puncture wound. As the two kings continued to stare at each other, Kord's body began to tremble. Beads of perspiration formed on his brow and scalp. Dizziness caused him to stumble slightly. The pain struck. Searing agony. His flesh consumed within a living, invisible flame. He wondered if the dragon had decided to incinerate him upon some wild whim. Kord felt as though his body had been consigned to the eternal fire pit of the damned. He wanted to scream out, shout in agony to relieve the burning. The Nordic king's instincts compelled him to fall to the floor and roll in frantic desperation to extinguish the invisible flame. Within his mind he found the strength and discipline to force down the panic and to endure the agonizing torment. The warrior suffered the fire in silence. Torrents of sweat rolled off his forehead, his hands clenched into tight fists and an occasional tremor shook his body. Every nerve ending pulsed, throbbing with agony. Kord's body endured severe muscle spasms as human DNA was rewritten and recombined to accommodate the dragon's unique genetic code.

Kord opened his mouth in a silent scream as his skeletal structure crackled and popped under the direction of the dragon genetic cocktail. His body radiated a bright greenish white hue and his eyes seemed to burn internally with the same fire. As he opened his mouth again, he screamed, not the scream of a human man in agony, but the roar of a dragon. The aura continued to surround his body, increasing in size until it took the silhouette of a male dragon. The man inside the green shade was barely visible. The green dragon of energy regarded Takeara with a look of respect before it dissipated, dissolving back into a shapeless mass. Within the space of five more heartbeats, Duncan Kord, Nordic warrior and king, stood, his body visibly stronger and his eyes glowing green with an unknown internal flame. Kord took two steps then stumbled. He caught himself quickly and slowly dropped to one knee.

Terrel and Saulle looked on in astonishment at the transformed human.

"Are you unwell?" Saulle asked.

Kord stood up slowly, shaking his head and blinking his eyes several times. "I'm fine. It felt like I was in the pit of the damned for a while."

A slender jill landed close to Kord and presented him with a small gold chest. Kord accepted the gift graciously. He could feel a deep bond of kinship with her. He knew her dragon name, her lineage and her history. A sea of information about her flooded his mind. The most distinct thing he reacted to, however, was her scent. His senses had increased dramatically. He could hear the drips of water falling off the stalagmites that adorned the cavern ceiling. He could sense the slight draft that blew through the cave regulating the temperature.

"Thank you, Chil'alea." He bowed his head slightly.

The slender female nodded her long neck and with one thrust of her powerful wings ascended to a nearby perch high in the rocky cavern.

Kord looked over at the Atlanteans. "I know all about her, all of them. It's as if I'd known them my entire life. Each memory, each family history is as clear to me as my own lineage. How can this be?"

"You have all the ancestral memories that Takeara possessed. This is your new home, Nordic king, and these are your kin," Terrel gestured to the dragons.

Kord opened the gold chest and lifted a large dragon medallion suspended from a heavy chain. The medallion glowed with an emerald-white brilliance, casting its light throughout the cavern. Kord placed the medallion around his neck and felt imbued with even more energy and vitality. "The amulet has great power."

"A symbiosis will form between your body and that medallion, Duncan Kord. Your enhanced body requires more energy than your human metabolism can provide. This amulet will aid your transition into a dragon and will allow you to perform amazing feats of skill and strength while in your human form." Saulle explained.

Kord studied the two beings carefully. Instincts told him there was something more, something they weren't telling him. Power seldom came without cost or consequence. "There is always a price or counterweight that balances eternity's scale. What is the price for these newfound gifts?" The new dragon lord steeled himself for the cost.

"Your body needs the energy supplied by the pendant in order for you to survive. You could not consume enough nourishment from the simple organic foodstuffs to sustain you. Also, the pendant's energy is constantly repairing and revitalizing your cellular structure and metabolism." Terrel read the confusion on Kord's face.

"You will be immortal. Your body will not age nor will it know death. Wounds will heal instantaneously and sickness will be eradicated as it enters your body. The price for immortality and being one with the dragons is you will be forever tied to the amulet you now wear. In time your body will adjust to its changes and be able to go for periods without rejuvenating itself, but at some point, you will have to energize your body with the power from the medallion. Our few remaining scientists were able to study the medallion and duplicate its properties to some degree, but the basic organic nature of the amulet is from their kind, not ours." Terrel pointed a willowy fingertip towards Takeara.

Kord looked over at Takeara. The elder bull slowly made its way toward the dragon cave's opening. "Where is he going?"

"He is leaving to begin his life of isolation. He has given you all the tools you require. The jills will assist you with your transformation and guide you with your other duties."

"NO!" The Nordic King moved swiftly blocking the old bull's path. He looked up at the great reptile and gently laid a hand on its large flank. "Takeara, you are a great king and a generous soul. Stay here, with your kindred, be a part of us. You said there are few of us left in the world, and I'll not condemn the only other male of our species to isolation. We are brothers. You've given me the greatest gifts any man could imagine. Stay here with me, brother! Lend me your guidance and wisdom. Help me." Kord pleaded gently but firmly. "There is no need for you to leave all you hold dear. In my mind you are still king. You've given me your knowledge, but not your wisdom and judgment, those are traits that can only be developed through time." Kord pleaded, "Stay with us and guide us forward. You are still a leader. We are stronger together."

Takeara's head lifted slightly. His dorsal armor stiffened and his eyes opened wide, as though he displayed pride. His facial expression softened as he regarded the Nordic king. The elder bull turned and walked back toward the large chamber. Kord followed quickly, greeted with several roars coming from higher in the cavern. It appeared that the jills heard and approved Kord's first decree.

Kord walked toward the two Atlanteans. "I owe you a great debt. You've revealed a part of me I'd have never known in my old life."

"We hope you will be happy here in your new life, Lord of the Dragons." Saulle replied.

"I have one request."

"If it be within my power." Saulle faced the new dragon lord.

"My sword, the last link to my human heritage and my forefathers. I have made the transformation but I still want my ancestral blade. I've done what you wanted, now, if what you told me is true, I should be able to take hold of the weapon with no ill effect."

"You will have much to occupy your time, dragon lord. Focus your energies there and we will return in sixty cycles with your sword. Is that acceptable?" Terrel proposed.

Kord nodded and turned toward Takeara. As he made his way toward the great chamber two young jills swooped down next to him, greeting him with bowed heads and gently growled. Kord instinctively stroked their powerful flanks, emitting a smooth rumbling cadence from his throat.

Terrel and Saulle waited until they were outside and a great distance down the pathway before speaking.

"The first part of our plan succeeded beyond our

expectations. He should have the dragons on the road to repopulation within a few generations." Saulle was visibly pleased with their success.

"Indeed, and with Takeara to guide him, he'll develop even quicker than we'd planned." Terrel nodded. "Let us hope that the other warrior is as accommodating to the beasts selected for him."

"Do you really believe we've mimicked the technology enough to succeed this time, Terrel?"

"It depends on the subject," the slender Atlantean began, "Our methods aren't as precise as Takeara's and the barbarian has no genetic tendencies toward the cats like Kord has toward the dragons. Duncan Kord was an anomaly, a one in hundred billion freak of nature. We're attempting to mimic such a rarity. The hormones and genetic replicators we've added to his food should allow Sagahr's genetics to meld with the Ciago Sabertooth's. The Ethiopian warlord will meld with the large native bears we discovered on the other side of the island."

Saulle nodded. "We will have a formidable defensive force in less than a decade's time."

"Indeed. The dragons will be partially repopulated and we'll have an army of tigers and bears to defend our lands from the human invaders in the interim. I assume we could impose upon Kord and his family should a desperate situation arise. After so many years, Saulle, we are close to accomplishing our goals."

The Rise of the Tiger
The End of the New Beginning
New Atlantis

Sagahr leapt from his medical bed. He landed instinctively on both his hands and feet. The position felt at once unusually natural and alien. The northern barbarian stood erect scanning his surroundings. Everything was white, a sterile glowing white that reminded him of the endless snow-covered mountains of Tibet and Mongolia. He moved cautiously, hands outstretched, probing for any wall or obstruction that would provide some contrast to the endless white sea. He kept inhaling large quantities of air, sniffing, searching for any trace or spoor carried upon the sterile air.

The barbarian paused as he considered his actions. His last memories were of battle. He'd been surprised by the Nordic king and disemboweled on the battlefield. "Kord," he exhaled a deep breath. "We killed each other in battle, both of us on our way to damnation. What kind of sorcery is this?"

Sagahr heard something. It was faint at first, but his senses quickly locked on the sound. He recognized the pattern and could feel each slight concussion against his inner ear. It was a heartbeat, a little rapid and irregular but it was a heartbeat. Sagahr felt his flesh tingle and something primal coursed through his body. He sniffed the sterile air again, confused by this instinctive reaction. He caught a small molecular trace and his eyes locked toward where his body knew the source to be. Cautiously he approached the source. Sagahr's body was partially crouched as he advanced, unlike any type of martial stance he'd ever used. His senses intensified, exhilarated at this type of stalk. He heard the impact of muted footfalls moving away from his approach. He wasn't alone! He followed the sound with his eyes and inhaled deeply, locking on the distinct scent as it carried throughout the disturbed air.

"I can hear you moving," he whispered just loud enough for his voice to be heard by the unseen adversary. "And I can smell you," the warlord added as he exhaled. Sagahr moved

51

rapidly toward the sound of footsteps, hands striking out with incredible speed toward his unseen adversary. Hungry fingers reached out, anticipating closing around an enemy throat. His fingers grasped only empty space. He heard the footsteps fleeing and he pursued, his senses honed in on the noise and he felt a surge of excitement at the chase. As he closed upon the noise, his body slammed into an invisible barrier nearly knocking himself unconscious from the force. Sagahr emitted an involuntary roar of frustration. The sound surprised and even frightened the warlord. The smell of his quarry was gone and he could no longer hear the muffled footsteps along the floor. Sagahr pressed his fingertips against the clear membrane and it crackled like lightning against his touch. The shock mildly stunned him and he quickly withdrew his hand.

"Cowards!" He spat the word with vile contempt. A powerful rage coursed through him and he threw a massive blow into the barrier. Blue static electricity from the unseen barrier intermixed with a dark yellow bioelectric surge from his body. The field wavered briefly and reformed. Only this time, Sagahr could sense increased power from the barrier and the sound of crackling energy was more audible. In a peak of anger, he threw several more blows into the invisible barrier. The barbarian's body emanated an amber-yellow glow as each of his blows increased exponentially in force. The barrier shimmered lightning blue as it strained to absorb each superhuman impact.

After a two-minute tirade of punches, Sagahr fell back exhausted. The warlord felt heaviness in his chest. Dizzying weakness permeated his body. He dropped to his knees breathing in heavy canine pants. Sagahr struggled to lift his head toward the direction he knew his captors stood, somehow unseen and protected. "What manner of hell is this?" He slipped into black oblivion.

Terrel and Saulle materialized outside the barrier staring at their unconscious captive.

"He is curt and savage," Saulle observed.

"Indeed. The transformation seems to have taken hold with no ill effect. We were wise not to give him the energy medallion yet. He has exhausted his limited internal metabolic fuel."

Terrel waived his hand and the barrier shimmered briefly and vanished. The slender Atlantean walked toward the fallen warlord and placed a yellow tiger medallion against his chest. The medallion glowed briefly upon contact and began transferring energy into the fallen warrior. "Just enough to keep him alive until he can be controlled."

"I will have a sedative line inserted into him as we did with Kord. We cannot risk him running rampant throughout the city." Saulle folded his slender arms. "We will try again when he awakens."

Sagahr awoke and rose to his feet. A lingering feeling of weakness caused him to stumble. The barbarian inhaled and exhaled heavily as he considered his situation. It was obvious he was a prisoner. How he survived the mortal wounds he'd received was a great mystery. He lifted the fur pelt around his waist and saw only unblemished flesh. His bowels and innards had been restored. No doctor in any of his lands could have performed such a feat. The barbarian took notice of a small square object attached to his right arm on the outside of his tricep. A thin clear tube on the tiny box penetrated his skin at the bend in his upper arm and forearm. He tugged at the tube and found it firmly embedded in his arm. He attempted to remove the box-like protrusion, which was also fused on his arm.

"The device is micro bonded to your flesh and cannot be removed by force without severe damage to your limb," a voice echoed around the chamber. Sagahr tried to pinpoint the location but the sound seemed to be everywhere. "Our voices are broadcast at several positions so you cannot locate us." The voice added as if reading his mind.

"Who are you?" Sagahr demanded. "Show yourselves!"

Two frail beings shimmered into existence. To the warlord they seemed no more than pre-pubescent boys. He walked toward them cautiously, eyes keen and senses extremely alert and focused. "Who are you? How did I get here?!" Sagahr was unaccustomed to captivity and not being in total control of any situation. The fact that two frail inferior physical beings had managed to capture and hold him prisoner was an unbearable affront to his manhood. He advanced toward them.

"Are you wizards? Sorcerers or demons?" Sagahr's nose detected a faint odor, a scent similar to an electrical storm. The barbarian halted his progress cautiously extending his hand. He could feel the barrier scarcely a foot in front of him. Instinctively, he knew his senses were far superior to what they had been. He reached out his index finger and touched the force field. Blue sparks danced and crackled around his finger but the arcs of energy didn't hurt him.

"We are none of those things, Sagahr, conqueror and slayer," Terrel began. "We are a peaceful race of beings that have brought you back to life to serve a noble purpose. It is not our wish to hold you captive, but your conduct has been rash and aggressive. Violence can't be tolerated within our city. Can you assure us that you will behave in a civilized manner? If so, you will be released."

"And if not," Sagahr challenged.

Terrel waived his hand slightly and the small box on Sagahr's arm whirred, a fluorescent blue fluid raced from the box through the clear tube and into Sagahr's blood stream. The barbarian immediately fell to his knees with fatigue and weakness. Terrel waived his hand again and the blue fluid stopped flowing. "We have no wish to keep you incapacitated, but we must insist you behave like a civilized being."

Sagahr stood slowly, feeling like a great weight had just lifted from his shoulders. "I give you my word, I will be peaceful." He mumbled, frustrated at his defeat. The thinner of the two beings waived his hand and the barrier around Sagahr shimmered briefly and vanished. The warlord cautiously extended his hand, half expecting another jolt. No shock came and he approached his captors.

"You have me at a disadvantage," Sagahr did his best to sound diplomatic, "You know my name and by the words you used to describe me, you know my history."

Before Sagahr could continue Terrel spoke. "We know all about you, Sagahr the Terrible, as your followers called you, or Barbarian or Conqueror as you've been called from those whose lands you've pillaged and whose women you've defiled." The slim Atlantean's disdainful tone marked him as a meek pacifist.

"I make no apology for who or what I am, wizard," Sagahr spat. "Conquest and war are a means of survival for my people. My ambitions are simple: kill and conquer as much as possible, demoralize the defeated, and steal their treasures while earning the loyalty of my followers and expanding my power base. It's a dangerous life, not for the timid. The rewards and pleasures are great for those bold enough to embrace it." Sagahr wrinkled his brow. "I won't live the life of a timid field mouse, waiting to be devoured by the hungry owl or jackal. I will be the predator and I will be the survivor."

"Yet you fell in battle and had to be saved by us."

Sagahr closed his eyes and nodded once, conceding the point. "I misjudged an adversary and paid the ultimate price for my folly." The barbarian shifted his powerful shoulders. "I have no use for this womanly chatter. It's obvious you healed my wounds and brought me to this place for a reason, so let us bargain." His face adopted a wolfish grin. "What do you want of me and what are you prepared to pay?"

The two Atlanteans stared at each other, Sagahr knew he had them off balance. "It was a simple question."

"We have need of a warrior with your skills and ruthlessness to lead a most unusual army," Terrel began. "From what little information we can still glean from the outside, we've learned that a large raiding party of Arabic warriors is massing in an effort to occupy this land. They've conquered the lands of Mesopotamia and are currently ravaging Egypt and the surrounding lands. They've sent out scouting ships and have stumbled upon our island nation. We have no real defensive capability nor do we have enough weapons or even citizens remaining to counter this threat. The very concept of war is repulsive to our kind. We have need of an army dedicated to the defense of this island and a general capable of leading such a force. We have chosen you for this purpose."

Sagahr paced back and forth considering what the frail beings had just told him. An opportunity to lead an army was appealing, but these puny creatures could be felled by a slight sea breeze. They were hardly soldiers. And they admitted their numbers were sparse. Sagahr wondered what kind of fools these wizards were. They admitted weakness to a stranger, and freely confessed to being pacifists. These beings were no more than sheep. Yet these sheep had effectively penned him up and could neutralize him with a simple wave of their hand. "And what do you offer for my services as general for your army?" The warlord bargained. "Can you pay in gold, jewels, women?"

"No," Saulle answered visibly recoiling. "We pay you with your life, your freedom and the opportunity to live in relative peace and tranquility save for when our home is threatened by outside forces."

"Training an army takes time; months and sometimes years of hard work and conditioning," the warlord responded. "If all your people are similar to you in stature, I have scarce hopes of making a fighting force from your ranks. The Arabs – if they've discovered your homeland – will arrive here in droves. They're conquering in the name of their prophet," Sagahr warned, examining the box fused to his arm. "Nothing is more dangerous than a man fighting for a religious belief whatever the god he serves."

"Two ships arrived several months ago. Many of their scouting party met untimely deaths due to some of our more aggressive wildlife," Terrel answered. "The others managed to escape and we've learned once they finish with Egypt and the surrounding territories, they'll focus their efforts here. We have no desire to be invaded."

Sagahr exhaled heavily and involuntarily flexed his biceps. His eyes were cold and calculating as he weighed the possibilities of the proposition laid out before him. "Peace and tranquility are of little value to me. The idea of slaughtering some religious fanatics, however, does interest me." The warlord nodded his head as he resolved his mental calculations. "Ten chests of gold and jewels and five slave girls and I'll agree to inspect this so-called army you have. If I see potential in the ranks I'll agree to train and command them."

Terrel shuddered. "We have no access to female concubines, warrior, but can provide you the treasure you desire and more. If that is what you require."

Sagahr looked over at his captors. "It is what I require, and remove this." He gestured toward the device on his arm. "You have my word you'll come to no harm. Consider it a gesture of trust and goodwill as we go forward with our alliance."

Terrel and Saulle stared at each other for a moment, reluctant to release their only hold over the barbarian. For several seconds the two Atlanteans remained silent. Finally, with a slight waive if his slender arm, Terrel removed the device. Sagahr absently rubbed the patch of skin where the device was a scant second ago, even more amazed at the magic these frail beings possessed.

"Show me this army," the warlord commanded.

Sagahr marveled at the majesty that was New Atlantis. Unlike Kord, he didn't question his surroundings or show any interest in the people he saw moving about the city. The warlord was busy gathering information like an army scout. Experience told him he was observing a dying nation. Wild vegetation encroached upon the titanic structures and several of the structures, though magnificent in size and scope, were in dire need of repair. It seemed the beings that inhabited this magical kingdom lacked the ability to control or even maintain it. He followed his guides to a sleek, cylindrical craft and stepped inside. The two Atlanteans fussed over a series of controls and the vessel rose into the air and began flying over the forest canopy outside the city.

"Incredible!" Sagahr stared out the forward viewer dumbstruck as the craft flew nimbly, dancing over the treetops. "What manner of power allows this thing to fly without wings?"

"Gravimetric waves," Saulle answered still focused on the craft's navigation panel. "The ship emits a wave pulse that repels attraction between objects of mass. In this case, the craft and the surface of this planet. By controlling these waves and directing them throughout the ship we can achieve flight without the need of forward velocity or the lift required by winged creatures."

"How fast are we traveling?" Sagahr marveled at the speed in which treetops passed under the craft.

"One third the speed of sound," Terrel replied. The Atlantean smiled briefly as he saw the confused look on

Sagahr's face. "About twenty times faster than any human warship is capable of achieving under full sail," the slender being added in terms the warlord could understand.

"By the Ancestors!" Sagahr marveled as he calculated the craft's forward velocity.

"We're preparing to land," Saulle announced after several more minutes of travel. "We're on the western-most edge of New Atlantis. Your army inhabits this area. It will be up to you to train them."

Sagahr followed his hosts off the sleek craft surveying the small clearing that served as a landing bay. They were surrounded by dense jungle and the sounds of wildlife dominated everything. Terrel produced a green object from inside his clothing and slid a fingertip across the top of the device. Sagahr heard a sharp whining sound that seemed to captivate him. Within the jungle he heard several roars and growls.

"Our army approaches," Terrel pointed toward the distant sounds.

As if on cue, the largest cat Sagahr had ever seen emerged from the dense jungle and entered the clearing. The beast was easily fifteen feet long with massive fangs.

"You idiots!" Sagahr cursed, "You'll only bring about our deaths!"

"No!" Terrel countered forcefully. "They will not attack, Sagahr. Look deep inside yourself. We have made you a part of them. Feel the feline creature within you. Remember when you were confined inside the force shield. You could sense things and hear things that would not be possible for a human man. We've made you more than just a man. You are a part of them. Call upon that energy, the power that now resides inside you."

Sagahr studied the great cat. Three more of the feline creatures emerged from the dark jungle. Something inside the barbarian responded to these creatures. He could smell their individual spoor. He could hear each breath they took and sense their intent. Sagahr felt the raw unchecked power each creature possessed, the drive to hunt, kill and conquer, so similar to his own barbarian nature. The barbarian let out a deep-throated growl, surprising himself as the sound radiated throughout the clearing. The four cats responded with thunderous roars that dominated the noisy jungle.

Terrel produced the tiger medallion and handed it to the barbarian. "This medallion will feed you and allow you to live as one of them, Sagahr. This medallion will give you the energy to live forever and to transform into one of them, only larger and more powerful. Become their ruler and lead the feline army of Atlantis. Put on the medallion, Tiger Lord, and take your place as leader of these great creatures."

Sagahr took the medallion but was still transfixed on the titanic cats. As the medallion touched his powerful chest it glowed, bathing him in a yellow nimbus. His eyes changed, becoming more feline than human. The barbarian fell to his knees. His body convulsed in spasms of agony. The ominous crackling sound of bone sliding against bone within his frame made both Atlanteans shudder. Sagahr shrieked. Pale, peach-colored flesh sprouted orange and black fur covering his powerful forearms. The warlord cried out, hands grasping his skull in a desperate attempt to calm the burning firestorm within. His jawbone crackled protruding forward, expanding along with his nasal cavity. Razor sharp incisors protruded from his mouth. Sagahr's screams of pain became hisses and angry growls. He fell forward on his hands, his body expanding, bursting through his clothing and leather armor. Amber and black fur covered his ever-expanding body. Within sixty seconds the man that had been Sagahr was no more. A massive feline creature with glowing yellow eyes replaced the human. Deep inside the tiger's chest, the medallion burned yellow, still visible to the naked eye, fueling the metamorphosis and providing the great beast untold power and energy. Sagahr's feline self was much bigger than the four other cats. The four felines acknowledged their new leader and assumed submissive postures. The cat that was Sagahr looked skyward and roared. The sound was one of defiance and challenge. A new master had come to the jungle. The four other cats roared acknowledging their new leader and turned off into the jungle.

Sagahr watched them leave and looked back at the Atlanteans. The cat closed its eyes and transformed back into human form. Sagahr wrapped the shredded clothing around his waist. The tiger medallion burned fiercely, engulfing him, as it continued to feed him newfound power and energy. The northern warlord flexed his muscles and as he did, his body glowed even brighter. He looked at his frail hosts and laughed.

"You have given me much, wizards," he flexed powerful muscles. "I'll give you an army of beasts that will conquer the entire world."

"We have no desire for conquest. We just want to be left undisturbed by the savages that are the new human race," Saulle replied.

"We will deliver your treasure at the next sunrise," Terrel added.

"Agreed!" Sagahr was still fascinated by the newfound power coursing through his flesh, "But the gifts you've given me are far more valuable than gold and jewels. You've given me power."

"Use that power wisely and live out your life in peace and prosperity," Saulle remarked as both Atlanteans turned toward their craft.

Terrel glanced back over his shoulder and watched Sagahr vanish, swallowed by the heavy jungle foliage. "I am beginning to question our logic with that one."

Saulle shook his head, "Our options are limited. Only three beings survived the augmentation. He is human," The frail being added condescendingly. "The power we've given him should suffice and he'll be duly occupied creating his army. His kind should be content with the simple primal pleasures found in carnage and conflict. When his kind land on our shores, bloodthirsty for conquest, we will be ready."

"We didn't tell him about needing to keep the amulet on to feed his enhanced body. And what about Kord? What will happen if the dragon lord and Sagahr discover each other alive? Will they not battle each other as they did before?" Terrel asked as he guided the craft back toward the city.

Saulle frowned, "Power is the ultimate aphrodisiac for that one. He will never take the amulet off. If he does, he will feel the ill effects in time and wear it again. Experience will be his teacher. As for Kord, they are at opposite ends of the island by design. Kord will be busy learning from Takeara and repopulating the species, we hope. Sagahr will be busy adapting to his new role and gathering all the territorial feline prides under his control – a task that should keep him duly occupied. Our third host will be stationed in the far caverns, if he survives. We've bought ourselves time, Terrel, and only farther along in time will we find our answers. We've done what is necessary to assure our survival and the survival of our dragon neighbors." Saulle watched the treetops whisk below the speeding craft.

Prelude to Annihilation
Dragon's Lair, New Atlantis

The slim craft gently landed in a small clearing several hundred yards from the dragon caves. Terrel and Saulle looked skyward as Takeara and another large bull performed breathtaking aerobatics. Both Atlanteans knew the other bull was Kord. The human-dragon hybrid was almost indistinguishable from his genetic sire. The only visible distinctions they noticed were Kord's short mane and pale-blond whiskers, a stark contrast to Takeara's ebony coloring.

"The human has done well." Saulle studied the creature through a magnifying device.

"Indeed," Terrel replied guiding a large covered box held aloft by anti-gravity units.

A sentry announced their presence as they set foot into dragon territory. Two slender jills soared overhead circling and inspecting the intruders.

"Something new."

"Indeed, it would appear Kord is applying security measures to this territory." Terrel observed as they walked along the narrow path.

Both beings approached the mammoth entrance to the dragon's lair. Duncan Kord, new Lord of the Dragons, greeted them. The Nordic warrior looked different; superhuman vitality radiated from his body.

"Welcome, my friends." He escorted them into the cavern eyeing the floating box with curiosity.

"It has been sixty cycles, Duncan Kord, and per our word we have returned with your sword." Saulle gestured over the box and it opened silently. Kord's ancestral blade lay suspended in the box tucked inside a modified leather sheath. Kord approached the blade cautiously and reached his hand toward the large pommel. He hesitated for an instant remembering the painful jolt he'd received earlier. His hand reached inside and firmly grasped the pommel, lifting the titanic weapon. With practiced grace, the lord of the dragons freed the blade and held it over his head. The altered steel gave off an eerie emerald glow bathing him in its light. He could feel energy coursing through his body.

"By Odin, the blade has fantastic power." Kord marveled as he swung the glowing steel in several fearful arcs and thrusts.

"It has the same properties as your medallion but can also give off great bursts of energy. You will learn to wield it in time," Terrel replied. "Use it with great care and wisdom as befits your position, Lord of the Dragons."

Kord sheathed the blade and slung the weapon over his shoulder, adjusting the straps and buckles. "I will, I promise."

The dragon king gestured toward a long stone foyer. "Come, let me return your earlier courtesy and show you my home."

The slender Atlanteans followed their host deep into the bowels of the dragon's lair. Kord showed them several nesting caverns hidden deep in the earth.

"We're several hundred feet below ground," Kord began. "I wanted the new hatchery deeper underground to take advantage of the warmer temperatures and better protection. There is a natural heat source here. Takeara claims an ancient volcano formed this land and the heat is a product of liquid rock inside the earth – the same properties as your original home it would seem. "

Terrel and Saulle looked at each other, clearly impressed Kord remembered the scientific discussion they'd had months earlier. This was not the confused barbarian they'd known, this was a leader who bore himself with pride and confidence. As they rounded a corner, both beings saw several dozen large dragon eggs being tended to by a lone female. The reptile looked over at Kord and nodded, grunting softly toward him. Kord smiled and repeated the sound.

"Our next generation." There was a sense of pride in the dragon king's voice as he turned to face his Atlantean guests, like that of a proud father watching over his children.

"You were able to reproduce with no complications?" Saulle asked bluntly.

The Nordic man's face turned crimson at the bold question, "That information and ability was a part of my transformation."

He coughed uncomfortably. "It was a bit awkward at first but now I am bonded to the females in a way I never was with any woman, including my wife."

He gestured back toward the opening and left the nursery with the two Atlanteans following close behind. Kord spoke of his ambitions and plans for his new people. For the first time since his resurrection, the Viking king seemed happy to be alive.

"Takeara has taught me much in a short time, but there remains a great deal left to accomplish before we are whole again." Kord nimbly walked back up the passageway. "There are other dragon species in other lands, distant cousins, which I will seek out once our population is established. We will unite together and provide a haven for all our dragon brethren."

Saulle and Terrell looked at each other. "We were not aware of this."

Kord paused and turned toward them. "Indeed, there are many aspects of dragons that your people are not familiar with. There are several human lifetimes of learning to be had from Takeara and the others. I am fortunate to have the elder king here for guidance." Kord turned and began walking. The Atlanteans followed in silence.

"When do you anticipate being able to aid in our island's defense?" Saulle asked as they re-entered the large main chamber. Kord turned, gazing up at the dozen jills perched on the rock precipices. He then glanced over at his mentor.

"There are scarcely enough of us now to defend our own territory. Even when the new young are hatched, they will need several years of nurturing and guidance. We aren't soldiers, we seek no conflict. We can barely patrol our own territory as it stands.

"You are not soldiers but yet you speak like a general. You have sentries flying throughout your territory even now. If there is a threat to Atlantis, can we call upon the dragons for aid?"

Kord glanced over at his mentor and the regal dragon nodded once. "I will answer your call myself if needed with whatever additional dragons that can be spared." Kord unsheathed his great blade and held it loosely in his hand. The weapon crackled and burned with power. "I sense unease. Is there a threat to our land?"

"No," Terrel replied quickly. "None that we are aware of – just rumors at this point. You have much to accomplish here, dragon lord. We will no longer keep you from your duties. We promised you the return of your ancestral blade at this time and we have kept our word."

Kord swung the weapon fiercely several times, reacquainting himself with the feel and balance of the sword. "You have at that. I am grateful."

Kord watched as both beings departed his home. Takeara rose and approached him. The great reptile gave off a series of soft grunts and hisses. Kord nodded and stepped over to a large rock outcropping. With a mighty swing of the sword, sliced the rock cleanly in two.

"I agree, brother, they are hiding something... their very bodies spoke of it. Have they ever inquired about using dragons as a defensive force before?"

More hisses answered his question.

"Something isn't right. Our Atlantean neighbors are scheming, and nothing good can come of it. I'll have Kayanna and Satarra keep watch on the coast. They have the sharpest eyes for spotting trouble. If they fly high enough in the morning thermals, they'll be able to see most of the eastern coastline. In the meantime, we have our own problems to deal with. Kord began speaking in the dragon tongue as both headed toward the hatchery.

"You were unwise to bring up defense at this point."

Saulle shook his head in disagreement. "We had touched upon it when we first reanimated the Viking. He is the only one who has truly been adapted to the alternative DNA embedded in his body. The serum from Takeara is something we could not duplicate perfectly. We did what we could to mimic its components, but our serum lacks some of the more complex chemical properties. The Viking has a dragon heart. Takeara sensed him. Our soldiers have been forced into a genetic manipulation and don't share the same bond with their host species."

"We've done what was necessary to preserve our lives and our dragon brethren. Our methods, though questionable, are for a greater cause, Saulle. We cannot turn back or change our course now. Our human soldiers and their animal counterparts are in place and we can focus back to more peaceful pursuits. Let us hope this is the last time we will have to partake in these sordid affairs."

Saulle waved his hand over the controls and their sleek craft banked toward the western coast of their island. "Our last subject should be fully integrated with his animal counterparts. One final check and we can focus on revitalizing our city."

Duncan Kord, Dragon Lord of New Atlantis stared out over the vast ocean from the highest peak of his mountain home. The stiff, cool sea breeze reminded him of his homeland and his past. Seven years transpired since the fateful events that altered his life. The sounds of young dragons riding morning thermals under the scrutiny of several matrons drew his gaze skyward.

"*My children,*" he thought holding up fierce dragon claws instead of human hands. "*Not exactly what I had in mind, but more than I'd ever hoped to achieve.* "

A thunderous roar broke the tranquil scene as an older jill descended toward their cave at fantastic speed. Kord recognized the alarm call and the swift moving dragon: Kayanna. Something alarmed the normally stalwart matron. The other dragons banked sharply, spilling air from their wings, descending toward their cavern. Kord spread his massive wings and leapt from his perch. His wings beat three times, then flared open while he circled down gracefully. With keen dragon vision, the young lord scanned his territory for any threat or danger. *Nothing. I see no danger. what could have spooked the matron?*

Kord tucked his wings and banked toward his cave. His body shot forward at breakneck speed. Seconds before impacting the ground, Kord opened his wings and arched the powerful appendages, catching large quantities of air. The drag slowed his descent. He gracefully landed and quickly entered the cavern.

There was a cacophony of voices. In his dragon form he fully understood each delicate cadence of a growl or hiss.

Kayanna was reporting to Takeara. *Many humans have arrived in seafaring vessels, they are under attack by packs of wild tigers.*

Wait until Kord is upon the throne! Takeara scolded her.

Kayanna bowed her head at his rebuke.

Kord quickly took his position beside the old king. *Forgive my tardiness. I was on the mountaintop watching the children, my brother. Kayanna may report to you as well as to me. We are partners in this undertaking ... your wisdom still far exceeds mine*

Takeara nodded. *Old habits and tradition my brother.* He turned toward Kayanna, his look much softer. *Continue, matron.*

Three vessels and many humans! They are trapped on the beach engaging several dozen large cats. I have never seen cats behave in this manner!" Kayanna looked up at Kord. *The humans may all be dead by now, my lord.*

Kord willed himself to return to his human form. He reached behind the large basaltic throne. Grabbing his discarded clothing and armor, he dressed himself quickly. He carefully buckled his scabbard and turned back toward the dragons. Only drip of distant water echoed throughout the voluminous cave as the dragons silently watched him.

Kord took a deep breath. *Kayanna, you will carry me to the conflict and drop me off nearby, then take to the skies and await my call.* He gestured to another mature jill. *You will accompany us. Circle high overhead and don't allow yourself to be seen. When Kayanna takes flight after dropping me, you will stay by her flank. When you hear my call, be prepared to attack!*

Is it wise to interfere in affairs not of our own? Takeara asked.

I sense trouble. My gut is in a knot right now, brother. Something is afoot and I can't get my bearings on it. I don't want our people embroiled in any conflict but I also don't want to see shiploads of people slaughtered needlessly. If these humans are here for peaceful purposes, so be it. If they are here to be aggressors, I'll handle them myself. I owe them at least a chance before they're slaughtered.

Takeara stared at his human counterpart, his great head tilted in confusion. Kord laughed as he mounted Kayanna's back, *Instinct. A human failing my brother. We shall return within half a cycle.*

Kayanna flew rapidly to the coastline. Kord's dragon sight spotted the conflict. At least ten men were down and three others were being mutilated by the largest cats he'd ever seen.

"By Odin, what manner of beast are they? Those men are being butchered." Kord then switched to the hiss and growl of the dragon language as spoken by his human vocal chords. "Set down in that nearby clearing, then take flight. Hopefully I won't require your aide."

The matron dropped from the skies, landing quickly in the small nearby clearing. As soon as Kord dismounted, she was alight again, quickly vanishing into the sky using the bright sun as natural camouflage from those on the ground. Kord unsheathed his sword and exhaled sharply as a fresh stream of power flowed through his body. He ran in superhuman bounds into the clearing toward the melee. With a war cry, he vaporized a large feline with a blast from his sword. Before the beasts could react, he was amongst them, swinging his battle blade in great arcs. Five cats attacked him in unison and Kord was pressed to defend himself. He found himself awash in fangs and claws. He severed one paw with a short upward swing and followed that motion with a lunge thrust, shearing the breastbone of another feline. A hot pain scalded his senses as a large forepaw sliced into his unprotected thigh. Kord summoned more reserves. His body radiated energy as the dragon medallion fed him more power. His strikes and parries were blinding, beyond the ability of the cats to avoid. The large beasts roared with outrage and momentarily fell back to reassess their new enemy. Three more cat corpses littered the battlefield and two others limped away hemorrhaging blood and sinew from gaping wounds. Kord held his mighty sword aloft, pouring more energy into the weapon so that it glowed like an emerald star.

"I am Duncan Kord, son of Odin, last of my line and Lord of the Dragons!! Be gone hell beasts!"

The surviving humans retreated to their beached ships and fired several volleys of arrows into the retreating feline aggressors providing Kord an opportunity to fall back. The Viking warlord took a moment to assess his situation. The gaping wound on his leg was little more than a scar now. Normally after such exertion he'd be winded, borderline exhausted and panting, but his heartbeat was still low and he felt no fatigue or battle weariness. He lowered his weapon and glanced back at the humans he'd just saved. He understood their looks of stark terror. The men were probably as much afraid of him as they were of the feline attackers.

Kord judged them to be Middle Eastern, possibly Egyptian or from somewhere in the southern-most continent due to their dark coloring. "Have no fear!" he spoke in broken Greek, hoping one of them understood the language. "I am not your enemy. But as you can plainly see, this is not an island to be colonized or invaded. You would do well to tell any others who would dare venture here that only death bids them welcome by all manner of horrible beast."

A loud growl echoed through the nearby jungle and the scattered cats formed up in a scrimmage line. Kord's jaw fell open in amazement. These animals were responding to a sentience commanding them. Foliage shuddered, then the biggest cat Kord had ever seen stepped into the clearing. Its eyes glowed a bright yellow, burning like twin setting suns. Several yards from where the cat emerged, an equally large black bear with massive fangs appeared and then stood on its hind legs. Easily twenty feet tall, its eyes burned the color of red rubies. Another dozen smaller bears emerged from the jungle to join with the felines.

"Great Odin! They're working together!"

Kord heard the stunned murmurings of the men behind them. "Ready your bows!" he shouted in Greek, praying they understood.

The largest cat stepped forward and studied him. Kord raised his weapon and prepared himself for combat. His instincts took over and he moved his blade in a defensive motion as the great cat fired twin searing yellow energy beams

from its eyes. The beams struck the blade and were deflected
back toward the cat, scalding the sand several feet in front of
him. The massive bear launched his own assault of searing
ruby lances from its eyes. Kord's sword parried those beams
and he retaliated with a burst of pale green fire from his blade.
The beasts adroitly dodged his blasts and fired again. Kord
screamed a battle cry and charged forward, his sword a blur,
parrying dozens of yellow and red beams. The smaller
creatures formed a defensive blockade and Kord slaughtered
several before withdrawing amidst a tight maze of energy
beams.

The great cat turned its attention toward one of the ships
and fired. The timbers erupted in flame and the men scrambled
overboard to avoid being burned alive. Men aboard the other
two ships launched several volleys, filing the sky with arrows.
The bear incinerated dozens of shafts before they reached the
apex of their flight. The men aboard ship screamed in terror.
Kord fired several salvos from his sword, vaporizing cats and
bears. He managed to score a glancing hit against the gigantic
nimble feline leader. Kord took some small satisfaction as the
great feline's hind quarter smoked and sizzled.

The cat roared again and another dozen felines
materialized from the jungle. At least five more large bears
filled in the gaps Kord had cut in their line. The largest cat
walked forward. it paused and slowly began to change. It
shrank, becoming human in front of Kord's very eyes. More
panicked screams filled the air from the men behind him. The
man facing him pulled the remains of clothing around his
torso and turned to face the dragon lord. An unbridled hate
seized Kord and bile rose in his throat. The man seemed just
as angered and stunned as he recognized the human
adversary.

"You!" Kord shrieked with a venomous hate-filled
accusation.

"Nordic worm! I gutted you on the battlefield!"

"I'm going to vaporize you where you stand, barbarian!"
Kord pointed his sword toward his adversary.

"Do that and my associate will burn the other two ships
before you can stop him. Meanwhile, I'll unleash these and the
rest of my army upon you." Sagahr gestured toward the jungle.

"There are more of us, Kord, watching and waiting. Standard military tactics. Never deploy all your forces, only enough to get a job done." The barbarian growled and another dozen cats emerged from the jungle, staying well back from the potential fray of battle. "Have you forgotten?"

Kord raised his sword. The weapon burned unfettered with energy. Sagahr eyed the sword with interest. "It seems you've made the acquaintance of the same two wizards that gave me my power, only they were more generous with you." The warlord approached him, gesturing his army forward. "I will take this matter up with them in due time!

"After I've killed you, again, Kord, I'll study your weapon and keep it for myself."

Kord lowered his weapon and quickly sheathed it. "Let me introduce you to some new tactics, brute – the concept of air support!"

Kord roared into the sky and the battlefield fell silent for two heartbeats, then hell was unleashed as streams of amber and scarlet fire raked Sagahr's front lines. The animals broke rank as the two dragons swept back and forth over the line, spraying multiple volleys of fire. Two large bears fled toward the water, their black fur ablaze in crimson flame, howling in agony. In the background, Kord heard his old adversary cursing him.

Kayanna swooped in low and spilled her velocity by spreading her wings like parachutes. She quickly touched down, firing several blasts of fire toward the scattered creatures. The surrounding forest was now ablaze. The Nordic warrior leapt upon her powerful back and within two wing beats she was airborne again. Several red and yellow beams filled the air and Kord ordered his dragons to withdraw. He cursed aloud in frustration! What had the Atlanteans done? What in the name of Odin were they thinking, giving Sagahr a legion of monsters to command? Kord gazed back, and his dragon vision saw the billows of flame as the other two human ships were attacked. No doubt their crews were being brutally slaughtered.

"Take us home, matron. We dragons need to prepare for war!"

Takeara, Saulle and several other Atlanteans watched the bloodshed and carnage through a three-dimensional display. They watched in horror as Kord was forced to retreat and the remaining human survivors were slaughtered. What disturbed them the most was the fact that the cats fed on the captives. Shrieks of fear, agony and despair echoed throughout the sterile room.

'Enough!" Terrel whispered. "Deactivate the surveillance cameras. I can stomach no more of this barbaric bloodshed!"

"He is savage," Saulle commented, almond eyes glaring at the floor. "We knew this to be when we augmented him. We cannot be shocked that the barbarian behaved according to his instincts. Plus we've given him the genome of our island's greatest predator. He is what we made him to be, a killer."

"We have a bigger problem, brothers. They are now aware of each other's existence. Both warriors have god-like power to command and we have provided them armies to continue their personal conflagration here, on our home. We cannot hope to stop either of them should they turn on each other."

Saulle and Terrel faced the being who had just spoken. "Then we must carefully observe both sides and give warning if either gathers their forces for an attack."

"This was not supposed to happen. Why would they destroy their fellow humans before even speaking with them?" Saulle pondered aloud.

"They are human. Who can understand why such a savage race does anything?" Terrel leaned heavily against a control console, pale with sickness from the hideous display of savagery. "I fear we made a huge mistake, my brethren and sisters. We put our faith in humans."

Duncan Kord, Lord of the Dragons, paced back and forth in the main chamber of his home. His hands were closed fists, knuckles white from his tension.

"I want patrols flying over our territory every few hours. Have the younger jills stay close to the cave. No more foraging into the woodlands. If they need more sustenance than our food stores can provide, they can fly out to sea and fish."

Takeara watched his enraged disciple issue commands in between his aggravated pacing back and forth. The elder bull had seen enough and decided to intercede.

"*NO!*" he hissed forcefully, startling both Kord and the other dragons. "*We cannot allow ourselves to become embroiled in a conflict with humans, Atlanteans or even augmented humanoids.*"

Kord spun toward the large bull. "You don't understand what this man is capable of doing? He slaughters for pleasure, killing is recreation to him. He is a danger not only to us but to all those that inhabit this island," Kord replied in human tongue.

"*This is not our fight. We have been betrayed by the Atlanteans. They took a small sample of my serum that was only to be used on your sword and perverted it into something else to create the monstrosities that now inhabit this land. We will no longer pay heed to the race of men – Human or Atlantean. They have proven themselves untrustworthy. Our duties to our young and our responsibilities to the other matrons should be the only things we need concern ourselves with.*"

"No!" Kord screamed. "He is an animal, a blight on humanity! He killed my wife! He killed my family and he killed my people. Now he's here, with more power than any man should have!" Kord smashed his fist against a large boulder. It crumpled under the force of his blow.

Takeara and the other dragons fell silent. One by one they turned away. Takeara spun his head back toward Kord and hissed, "*You too, are human, Nordic man, and you too are proving yourself unworthy of the great power given to you. You are one of us, but perhaps you are still too human to lead us.*"

"And you are naïve for all your great wisdom. You fail to recognize a threat to your very existence when it is right under your nose, my brother." Kord picked up his sword and made his way out of the cave, his frustration and anger palpable to all in the dragon community. He spun back quickly, facing the old bull. "Heed my words, all of you, this man will not rest until he controls everything on this island, including our territory! He will not stop until we are all subjugated or slaughtered!"

Duncan Kord, Lord of the Dragons, Viking chieftain and Nordic king stalked away and sat alone on a cliff edge staring up at the full moon that dominated the evening sky. The sounds of waves crashing upon the rocky seashore comforted him a little but his somber mood refused to fall away. What had been a dream was now a horrible nightmare. Sagahr was a danger neither the Atlanteans nor the dragons understood. Violence was foreign to the tiny beings and the dragon philosophy was one of strict non-involvement in the affairs of other races. Their philosophies would eradicate both races.

You stare outward when the problem is clearly not there, but inside our home, my king. The gentle voice whispered in his head.

Kord turned to see Kayanna approach, her regal neck bowed in a show of submission. Kord bowed his head and tapped the ledge next to him signaling the matron to join him. She gracefully settled next to him and followed his gaze starward.

"I know, matron. Sometimes I just like to look up at the heavens and ponder. The vastness makes me feel ... insignificant, an appropriate feeling given the current turn of events." Kord hissed and growled softly.

Takeara was unnecessarily harsh. He is afraid you will lead us into conflict. Is that your intent? To have us embark on a war when we are so few?

Kord looked up at her, gently patting her powerful flank. She nuzzled the top of his head with her jaw. Kord could sense her compassion and concern for his tenuous position. He was caught between his two halves. Should he attack the man who took his prior life, as any human would be more than justified in doing, or let that part of him go and lose himself in his new role? Kord stood, drew his sword and stared at the alien metal and the intricate designs etched in the lower half of the weapon.

Let strength and power be balanced by compassion, Kayanna's voice echoed in his mind. Then she spoke aloud. *"That is the message on your sword. Everything needs balance, my young king. You have the strength, courage, and power. We all see that in you.*

But, do you have the compassion to temper these things? One side of your sword has the etchings for strength and power, the other side, the etchings for wisdom and compassion. Two quantities for the scale. These are qualities you must utilize as you rule ... using only one edge and not the other will lead to ruin, like your sword. There must be a perfect balance."

"I understand. Seeing Sagahr brought up memories I have not yet been able to bury. The wounds have not fully healed from my other life, matron. I, too, was out of line earlier. This is not an affair of dragons. Our family cannot afford a conflict with those creatures right now or ever. As Takeara so wisely said, it is not our affair."

"Wise words, my king. May I convey them to the others?" she hissed and grunted softly. The matron stood, towering over him, *"I will leave you to watch the stars."*

"I will address our dragon kin. They need to hear these words directly from me. I am no longer concerned with humanity, though I still be part man. I am Duncan Kord, Lord of the Dragons ... that is who I am now, who I will always be." Kord sheathed his weapon and walked back to the cave.

Kord placed his weapon behind the mammoth basalt throne and then willed himself to change. He felt the raw unbridled power flow throughout his body as skin magically turned to scale armor. The great blond dragon let out a fierce battle cry summoning all to his side. Though Takeara acted like the king, all the dragons knew that role had been passed down to Kord.

Within seconds, the twenty remaining mature dragons and Takeara were in the massive main chamber. Several of the first hatchlings accompanied two of the younger jills that were tending the nursery. Two of the slim hatchlings scrambled up to the king, bowing their heads respectfully, before launching themselves playfully into the air, darting and swooping about almost like human children raptured in the joys of youthful play. Kord noticed that Takeara stood back, away from them. Kord gestured toward the old male to take his customary place by his side. Takeara moved forward cautiously and Kord nodded respectfully to the ancient bull. The elder nodded back and stood proudly by his side. Kord hissed once to silence all and began.

"*I am your leader,*" he began. "*Does anyone here challenge?*" Silence was the only response. "*You deserve a leader who cares only about what is best for you and I lost sight of that for a brief moment. Takeara is right; we cannot have any more contact with man or humanoid. What occurs around us is no longer my concern, unless it directly impacts our lands. You are my kin. We have much work to do, many lost brethren to find and more of us to raise*" he grunted softly and a small hatchling settled upon his mighty shoulder. "*These young ones are our future. We cannot battle without risking them. I will not do that. We shall not fight but we will watch and be wary. There is much for us to accomplish my brother and sisters. There will be no war, not on my watch.*"

The dragons were silent for several seconds, then erupted in a series of approving roars heard throughout the entire island. Takeara looked over at Kord and nodded his head in approval, that one gesture erased all the tension and doubts. Kord had made his decision, the only decision he could make.

One Son's Betrayal
Dragon's Lair, New Atlantis

Several years had passed since Kord's encounter with
Sagahr. The dragon king did his best to occupy his mind
with duty and responsibilities to his 'people' but there
was still that sixth sense, that all too human omniscience
telling him all he loved was in jeopardy as long as Sagahr, the
tiger lord, existed. Kord had flown over the far part of the
island on several occasions, studying the cats and the bears as
well. Both animal clans seemed to function separately for the
time being. The number of felines, however, seemed to be
increasing drastically. Whenever he tried to get closer, the
cats would roar in alarm forcing him to fall back. Sagahr had
feline sentries posted high in trees and at higher elevations.
The warlord had learned from their earlier encounter. Still,
every month or so since the initial conflict, the dragons
watched from the sky and let themselves be seen circling
high upon the thermals. The cats and bears had the ground,
but the dragons had the air and from that vantage point
could see everything. More importantly, Kord wanted Sagahr
to know he was watching him and on the alert. If Sagahr
believed Kord was prepared for war, it may be enough to
dissuade the tiger king from attacking his lands. Sagahr
thrived on surprise and Kord was doing his best to take that
element away.

An alarm cry ended the king's train of thought, snapping
him back to reality. A young jill glided through the cave,
landing gently in front of him. She bowed her slender head
before addressing him. "*A flying craft has landed on the outer
boundaries of our territory. It is the Atlanteans that were here before,
my lord.*"

"*Escort them here,*" he instructed as he changed into his
human form. It took Kord several minutes to become
reacquainted with his human limbs and dull senses. He had
been a dragon for so long it now seemed unnatural to
become a man.

Takeara watched him carefully, a confused expression on the old bull's face.

Kord laughed. The look was almost human – confusion. "Answers, my brother, let us find out what our deceptive guests want and ask our own questions in return. Information is always a good thing to have and I fear we have very little on what has been occurring on the other areas of our island home." Even the human language seemed to be forced from his vocal cords. Takeara and all of the other dragons had learned the human tongue but Kord rarely spoke the language anymore.

Kord finished adjusting his armor and was seated on the gigantic throne when the two Atlanteans were escorted inside. Kord detected their nervousness. All was clearly NOT well. "I had expected this visitation some time ago, after my encounter with Sagahr. Now, several years later you come to pay me a call?"

Silence was his only answer. The dragon king continued his soft rebuke. "It would appear you broke a trust with my people and deceived me as to your true purpose for giving me new life."

Again, only silence. Kord stood from his throne, casually picking up his sword and tugging it free of the scabbard. The metal glowed and the weapon crackled with innate power. As he approached the two slender beings they retreated nervously.

"You have no reason to fear me, Atlanteans. I had owed you a debt for my new life, but as for my people, you can never regain their trust." Kord stopped scant inches and looked down upon them. "Why are you here?"

Terrell stared at the Sword of Odin. The power inherent in the blade and in its wielder overwhelmed the Atlantean. "S-Sagahr paid us a visit shortly after your encounter, he demanded we provide him a weapon of equal or greater power to that which you carry."

Kord took a step backwards, considering his sword. "By the Gods! Tell me you didn't give him what he wanted!"

"We can't." Saulle replied. "We exhausted the remaining Uru metal and the other minerals used to re-forge your blade, plus the serum we had from Takeara had all been used in the weapon's forging process. We could only duplicate the base properties of the serum that created Sagahr and Timmeron."

"Timmeron?" Kord repeated the name. He had heard it before and his mind raced to recall the name. It came to him: 'Timmeron the Conqueror', the most lethal tribesman in the lower jungles of the southern continent. Kord exhaled sharply as he stepped closer to the clearly frightened Atlanteans. "Fools!!!! Do you know what you've done? Do you have any idea whom you've given power to? These are madmen, only concerned with conquest and slaughter! Why, why would you do this?"

"We have no means to protect ourselves, Kord. We had assumed that if we could take some of the fiercest human warriors, alter them, and offer them a peaceful existence they would be perfect defenders and soldiers. We can't understand what went wrong ... they should be content." Terrel mused.

"They are more barbaric animal than human," Kord spat. "They are corrupt, greedy, manipulative and power hungry. They have no value for human life or peace. They live only to pillage and plunder. You've created two demons to defend you and in turn have doomed yourselves to be enslaved by the very madmen created to protect you."

Kord paced, agitated, as the ramifications of what they had done rippled through the military knowledge still in his mind. "You have endangered all of your people and all of the dragons with your treachery. For all your great intellect and knowledge, you are pathetically naïve as to the darker underbelly of humanity!"

"We seek your aid, Kord and the aid of the dragons. We cannot meet Sagahr's demands, our attempts to stall and delay him further have failed. He has threatened to destroy us if we don't comply. If we could have your sword to study, perhaps we could find a way to mimic its power..."

"By Thor's Hammer!!!" Kord screamed. "Are you mad!! Have you not heard a single word I've said to you? You would give this demon even more power? What do you think he would do once he had a weapon? Leave you alone? No, he would demand something else from you of greater value knowing you would comply out of fear. I will not relinquish my ancestral sword back to you so you can attempt to place us all in even more danger. Besides, you have told me that the weapon can only be handled by me ... how would you be able to study a blade you cannot touch?"

"We would have to exhaust the weapon's power and store it in an environment void of any light or energy source from which the Uru metal could draw power. In that dark controlled setting, we could safely study the blade without fear of reprisal from the blade's organic defenses." Terrell shifted his posture, the tension visible as he spoke. The anger built up in the Viking king with each continued word of explanation. "If we could not duplicate or create a reasonable facsimile of your sword, we could give Sagahr your deactivated, virtually powerless weapon ... and once the weapon was exposed to light, he would never be able to use it because he could never touch the genetically encoded metal."

Kord shook his head in utter disbelief. "And what would happen once Sagahr realized the weapon you gave him was useless?"

Terrell and Saulle looked at each other. Their discomfort was obvious. Kord knew the answer and his stomach knotted at how far the Atlanteans were willing to go. Secretly he admired their bold plan, "You hope that the shock from holding the re-energized blade would be enough to kill him and that would solve your problem." Kord spun around and walked back toward his throne. He glanced over at Takeara and several other dragons. They watched their king with great interest wondering what he would do.

Kord placed his weapon against the throne and sat. "The shock would not kill him. If Sagahr is as strong as you've made me, the sword could harm him. But would he not heal as easily as I can?"

The Atlanteans nodded.

"Then you'd only succeed in angering him further. The barbarian would raze your city and slaughter you all for such a deception and I would never have my ancestral blade back." Kord sighed. The Atlanteans, for all their scientific advancements and claims of peace, weren't beyond deception and even murder. "I'm sorry. I can't help you." He gestured toward the rest of the dragon population. "We can't help you in this. Your folly is too great and too far beyond my ability to undo. I fear you have doomed us all. Our numbers are too few to engage Sagahr's and Timmeron's forces. If they come to your city you will have to flee. There are abandoned caves at the northwestern most tip of our territory. The thermal heat is negated by the cooler ocean winds making them unsuitable for us, but your people could find shelter there and perhaps safety." He glanced over at Takeara and the elder bull nodded, "That is all we can do for you at this time and it only delays the inevitable for both of our species."

Saulle and Terrell nodded, heads hung low, and slowly walked away. Kord shook his head in disbelief as he contemplated the stupendous atrocities they brought down upon them all. The dragon lord buried his head in his hands, sighing deeply as his hands slid over his eyebrows, by his ears and down his long blonde locks. Takeara looked on, not comprehending the human gesture.

"You are unwell?"

Kord looked up at his colleague, "Do dragons get headaches? Because right now I have one literally fit for a king"

Takeara tilted his head not understanding. *"I did not see you get hit, my brother."*

Kord managed a sudden laugh and he stretched. It still felt awkward being human after so many years. He looked at his hands, flexing them and watching the muscles in his forearm ripple. "We will be invaded, it's just a matter of time," Kord whispered so only Takeara could hear. "At the rate Sagahr's forces are breeding, they will exhaust their food supplies and forage deeper into other territory looking for prey. Game animals will naturally migrate away from Sagahr's territory further reducing the food sources and bring a shortage that much sooner. I can only assume that Timmeron's forces are also increasing their numbers. Mammals are able to procreate far quicker than our kind. We will be outbred and overwhelmed." Kord sighed again. "It's only a matter of time and numbers. We cannot fight against such overwhelming forces even with our superior strength and power of flight. Our Atlantean neighbors have doomed us."

Takeara's regal head sagged. *"I have had these same thoughts and have arrived at a similar conclusion. There is only one way to save our kin. We must flee. Let them have this island. We will find another home and they will be trapped here. They will consume every living thing here and then turn upon each other as they starve, trapped on this small land with no escape. Tigers cannot swim nor can they fly. Bears have the same afflictions. Let them have this place while we will find another. That is our only alternative, the only way we can survive.*

"And the Atlanteans?" Kord whispered, already knowing Takeara's answer.

"*The ever-meddlesome Atlanteans will have to flee as well. They are a society in decline, a small fractured piece of a once proud race ignorant in the ways of mankind and arrogant in their believed superiority. We cannot help them. I fear they doomed themselves the moment they altered those human barbarians. I will grieve because they did aid us in finding you. For that we will be eternally grateful.*" The elder bull paused, grunting slightly as a young hatchling swooped and darted through their corner of the cavern. The great monarch hissed gently and the hatchling flew off. "*We need to find shelter to protect our young from harm. I fear you were correct in your observation earlier. We are in great peril. There is a species of us that live in the highlands of the northern most landmass. They thrive on cold but there are large heated caverns there, much like the ones that were in our older home ... the Atlanteans called them 'geothermal pockets'. There is food for us there and shelter. Life will be a struggle but we will be alive to continue our race. Protocol demands we ask permission of the occupying race to settle. The Arctic Frost Dragons are few and should not object, but to avoid conflict we must ask. As our king you must fly there, find them and make our plea.*"

"And what if Sagahr attacks while I am away?"

"*Then I will be here, brother, and I will lead the defense of our home. My plasma glands and ocular beams are not as potent as your amulet-powered weapons but I can still generate enough heat to melt rock – more than enough to char feline hide if need be, as you witnessed during our first encounter. Your enemy has been busy and has so far not ventured here. We have no reason to believe that he will do so in the time it will take you to complete the journey.*" The elder lowered his head to eye level, "*You must do this if we are to survive. We must have a home and the northern lands are our best hope.*"

Kord hesitated. "Wouldn't you be a better representative to plead our case than me? I am a soldier, not much in the ways of dragon diplomacy."

Takeara shook his head, a sad look softening his regal face, "*You underestimate your abilities. Your amulet makes you not only stronger than I but faster. I would require more time to make such a journey. You can fly faster and farther without rest. Time is our enemy, more so than those cats and bears. We are on opposite ends of this land mass and it will take time for your human nemesis to cover such territory on foot. We will continue to watch and be wary. If we are invaded, we will fight as best as we can, then take to the air, riding the thermals landing only to rest the young in the sea cliffs.*"

"And our unhatched?" Kord grunted, angrily already knowing the answer.

"*Sadly, they would be lost. We could not defend the hatchery. Eventually we would be overrun while fighting a defensive war. You and I could deal, effectively, with the regular cats and bears, but the two enhanced creatures will take much power to defeat and we cannot afford to lose even one hatchling or matron. The matrons' armor is not nearly as thick as ours ... they can be hurt with less destructive force. The unhatched would be sacrificed to protect the living. It is a deep loss and a horrible price we would have to pay. Let us hope this will not come to pass.*"

"Takeara," Kord began solemnly, "I have learned not to challenge your wisdom, but if I am as powerful as you say due to this amulet, then it is safe to assume that Sagahr and Timmeron are equally enhanced. Would it not be more prudent if I stayed here to defend our territory and you make the trip despite the extra time it would take?"

The elder bull's mane drooped. "*On this island, in our group, I have status because you have decreed it so. In other dragon colonies I am an old, impotent bull, past his prime carrying no weight or authority. My position here is unique and unrecognized anywhere else. My young king, you are the only one who can make this trek. Other dragons will pay me no heed. You have the bearing of a king and will be recognized as such.*"

Kord realized what Takeara said was accurate. Old bulls were expected to live out their last years in isolation until they died. "Your wisdom and logic are annoyingly sound." Kord cracked his knuckles. "My gut tells me trouble is coming, brother. It's time for us to take action."

"*You must start the journey with great haste. The sooner we establish a new home the sooner we can leave this place.*"

Kord stood naked atop the seafaring cliffs under the bright afternoon sun. He raised his amulet up to the day star. A rush of solar power energized every cell in his body. The surge of energy was euphoric. His body bathed in an emerald green nimbus. Kord fed upon the amulet's energy until great torrents of power rippled through his body and arcs of power crackled and danced around his large frame. He reached down and grasped his sword, infusing even more energy into the blade's magical metal. The weapon glowed like its wielder. Kord sheathed the blade and placed it in a large satchel. The dragon king knew where he was going and now, he had the energy to make the flight as fast as his enhanced body could travel.

The dragon lord focused his will and transformed. Though he'd performed the metamorphosis many times, he still hadn't adjusted to the drastic changes between the sensory perceptions of each distinct species. Kord reached out with a large claw and tucked the satchel containing his sword, armor and clothing into the natural pouch between his wing and shoulder blade. The great reptile gazed over its massive shoulder, surveying its lands. With minimal effort, he unfolded each fifteen-foot wing. The wings caught the ocean updraft, lifting him into the sky. Kord flapped his large wings several times and soon sped northward faster than he'd ever thought possible. Time was the enemy now. He could only hope that Sagahr and Timmeron would not attempt to spread across the island until his return. The two kings could lead their dragons to a new home and a better life. Sagahr could starve and rot, trapped in isolation on the dead chunk of rock.

Kord spent three weeks looking for the frost dragons. He found evidence of a dragon society. The ice caverns appeared to have been vacated hundreds of years ago. He flew further north looking for more signs, but found no evidence of any kind. There were no volcanic caverns or geothermal pockets that he could detect. Kord hoped to find them further north but he was wrong. Takeara had described a cold environment with evergreen, rugged spruce trees and heavily furred animals and large, hoofed creatures wandering the large snowy plains. What Kord found was an endless plain of ice- and snow-covered flatlands and mountains with no signs of life. No species of dragon had been in these lands for centuries. The territory was an icy barren wasteland. They would all have to relocate somewhere else in either the southernmost continent or one of the island Saxon nations. They would have to coexist with humans until a suitable home could be found.

A sense of unease plagued the dragon king as he flew toward home. The human part of his makeup, the part that gave him instinct, told him there was trouble ahead. He'd had that inclination when Sagahr first invaded his Nordic kingdom, slaughtering and killing everything in his path. That sense of panic dominated his being propelling him forward at fantastic speeds. Kord pushed harder, focusing more energy into his wings. The dragon rocketed through the skies like an organic jet.

Ahead he could just make the outline of New Atlantis. Thick billowing clouds of black smoke hovered over the island. From miles out it was difficult to determine the exact origin. *FASTER!* He urged himself, consuming more energy from his amulet. Every instinct the dragon lord possessed screamed danger as he propelled himself ahead. The contrail from his velocity lit up the skies over the coast of New Atlantis. Kord executed a hard 10g turn as he banked and dove towards his home in the coastal caverns.

Corpses!! Dozens of bears and a handful of large tigers littered the coastline and woodlands of his territory. Their hides had been charred and eviscerated by dragon claws. Kord felt his heart tear as he spotted three dead jills, their armored hides torn apart and beautiful wings ripped from slender, powerful torsos. Kord's roar of outrage echoed throughout the mountains and carried throughout the island. Kord swept into the narrow cave entrance at breakneck speed, deploying his wings like massive air brakes, spilling velocity in sparse meters. He ran on all fours down the corridors toward the hatchery. He saw two dead young dragons – his first children – butchered. The matron raising the eggs was nearby, her head nearly decapitated from her body.

NO! Kord sobbed. His large reptilian head loomed over the crushed skull of the matron and destroyed dragon eggs. *Please, Odin, not twice, I beg of thee. not twice in a lifetime!* He prayed to his old Gods despite knowing they were fabrications of Atlantean wizardry. The scent of bears and cats assailed his senses, driving him into a rage. Kord raced back up the passage, the throne area had been ransacked, almost as if the foreign invaders had been looking for something. Several old artifacts had been obliterated and the once-regal throne had been defiled by bear scat and cat urine. *This is war, Sagahr! I know you're behind this. This time there will be no sneak attacks, I will kill you!*

Kord shot from the cave and winged his way toward the Atlanteans, keeping a lookout for his kin. Where were they? As he closed on the Atlantean's capital city, it was clear the titanic metropolis was ablaze. Thick, billowing smoke hung over the city like ominous thunder clouds. Kord could hear the screams of its citizens and the roar of dragons! He dove swiftly toward the sound and saw Takeara locked in combat with both Sagahr and Timmeron. There were scarcely a handful of matrons alive. Several dragon corpses and dozens of cat and bear corpses littered the battlefield. Kord focused his will and unleashed a searing blast with his ocular beams. Burning lances tore through Timmeron's flank setting the twenty-foot bear's flesh ablaze. Kord continued peppering several other opponents as he hovered over the warring species.

Before the dragon king could press his attack, Sagahr retaliated. Scalding yellow energy beams bore into his armored hide scorching his scales searing the flesh beneath. The stunning force of the beams slammed the dragon lord into the earth with a titanic impact. Kord felt the pain from the hard landing but recovered quickly. Before he could focus his senses to retaliate, the tiger lord charged, crashing into him like a battering ram. Sagahr's razor sharp claws tore into his hide and sharp fangs sank into his forearm. Kord turned and whipped his head forward sinking his razor-edged teeth into the tiger lord's spine hearing the satisfying crack of vertebrae. Kord kicked up his hind claws raking the tiger's underside. Sagahr emitted a roar of pain and surprise. The pain of Kord's bite caused Sagahr to release his grip. Sagahr fired his energy beams into Kord's exposed underbelly forcing the dragon lord to release his vice-like bite and fall back.

Sagahr limped away in retreat, still firing his yellow-orange beams, pushing the enraged dragon king back further. Both combatants paused as their hideous wounds miraculously healed. Kord could hear Takeara reengaging Timmeron while the few remaining jills continued to spray their amber and ruby flames. Kord tensed his massive pectorals, stimulating the plasma glands in his torso. An acidic taste filled his throat. He inhaled deeply, and then exhaled, spraying a stream of fiery plasma towards his nemesis. Whatever the plasma touched either exploded into flames or simply evaporated. Sagahr had taken the brunt of the blast. His fur was ablaze. The tiger wailed in agony and rolled frantically in the sand, desperate to extinguish the fire. Kord turned his attention to the remaining dragons. They were being pressed by the sheer numbers of attackers. He unleashed another searing plasma volley, sweeping his long neck in a 180-degree arc saturating the grounds in front of his allies with energy and creating a titanic wall of molten rock and fire.

The fire will not last long and the ground will harden again, he warned. *We cannot win this fight.* Kord was relieved to see that Kayanna had survived the battle so far, he had a special affection her. *Use the time to flee, leave this island, I will keep our enemies at bay as long as possible!*

Kayanna radiated frustration. *They came by sea, my lord.* she gathered her strength while she watched the sea of fire. *On a ship, one we thought destroyed. They arrived on our shore under cover of darkness. We fought them off as long as possible, but were forced to flee. The nursery….*

Gone, Kord replied sadly. *Our children are gone dearest matriarch, and I will make sure they pay for their horrid act with their lives!*

My lord, my fire is nearly depleted. Kayanna pointed her claw toward the diminishing wall of flame. *The other matrons are also depleted. We cannot maintain another sustained attack.*

Kord hated this defeat, but there was only one possible decision. *I know. You carry the next generation, Kayanna. You and the others must flee, find a safe haven and raise our young. Takeara and I will stay behind and end this bloodshed, Sagahr and his minions must be stopped here. if they leave this island all life, everywhere, is doomed. We will find you once the battle is done.*

Takeara had joined Kord and Kayanna. The elder dragon nodded in agreement. *FLEE MATRONS!* He barked. The aging bull focused his thoughts on Kayanna, *Kord's barrier diminishes and our enemies are gathering their strength.* The elder bull fired a sweeping ocular blast, driving back the first wave that tried to cross the diminished wall of fire.

GO! For our children! Kord pleaded firing another plasma burst.

The three remaining jills took to the air fleeing their home, heading north toward the sea.

Sagahr's army broke through the wall of fire and rushed the two remaining bulls. Kord was hard pressed warding off several attacking creatures. His foreclaws raked gaping wounds upon several bears while he used the needle-like barb in his tail to impale a charging tiger. He heard Takeara roar and hiss. Kord glanced over quickly to see the old bull engaged in heated combat with Sagahr. The large cat led four smaller felines in a group assault in an effort to overwhelm the large dragon. Kord could do little to aid his brother while he busily fended off Timmeron and six other bears. Sagahr was using standard divide and conquer tactics. The tiger lord had superior numbers and was marshaling his forces like a master tactician.

Kord fought on frantically, desperation accompanied each swing of his powerful forearms and snapping of his jaws. The enemy kept coming, an endless sea of tooth and claw. For each tiger or bear slaughtered, two more replaced the fallen. He glanced toward Takeara. The old bull was still in a heated battle with Sagahr and holding his own. Kord could tell the elder male was weakening. His last spray of fire was pale and lacked the normal potency. Kord spied three more tigers attacking the old bull's unguarded back. He roared a warning but was too late. Three more bears sank their teeth into Kord's armored flanks, forcing the dragon lord to worry about his own life. The dragon lord flapped his powerful wings lifting himself into the air. With a spiteful swipe he broke the jaw of a bear still clinging to his lower leg. The rays of sun bathed his body, rejuvenating him. Kord unleashed a savage volley of fire, vaporizing dozens of adversaries.

Takeara had fallen but was still flailing his hind legs and firing ocular beams at his adversaries. Sagahr blasted the elder bull with a searing burst of yellow plasma and sank his massive fangs into the bull's charred flesh.

NO! Kord's mind shrieked. The dragon lord spilled air from his wings diving toward his enemy. He opened his mouth and fired a titanic blast of fire. The ground around Takeara erupted in flame and nearby rock melted under the searing heat. Kord swooped over his enemy firing multiple salvos into the tigers and bears, driving them back. Sagahr's beam's slammed into his armor while he turned for another pass. Kord banked sharply, avoiding several more beams and fired another searing salvo of fiery plasma into the enemy's ranks. At some unseen command Sagahr's forces broke and retreated. Kord continued to pepper the retreating forces as they fled.

Seeing the lifeless, unmoving Takeara caused the dragon king to break off his attack. He landed quickly and approached the wounded bull.

The elder raised his head weakly acknowledging him. *I fear I will not see our new land, my brother. my life has come to an end.*

Kord's throat constricted with sorrow. *I'm sorry, Takeara. I couldn't hold them all back. I failed. We have been exterminated. Sagahr has taken everything important in my life for a second time.*

NO! Takeara replied weakly, *WHERE THERE IS LIFE, THERE IS ALWAYS HOPE. LEAVE THIS PLACE, BROTHER, WE MUST SURVIVE.*

Despite the elder dragon's words, Kord still despaired. *We have only three females left, all injured and weak, flying off to find a new home, not enough to start over.*

Takeara narrowed his gaze. *You must try, Kord, we cannot simply cease to exist, not after so long, to simply be exterminated is unthinkable.* The great bull struggled, taking in a deep breath, Kord could hear blood-filled lungs wheeze as Takeara struggled for air. *You were right earlier, we should have dealt with these enhanced beings after their attack on the shores. I did not understand as you did, this is my fault, had I not interceded for isolation we could have survived.*

Kord placed his forefoot on Takeara's shoulder. *No, Takeara.* The dragon king focused his thought directly to his mentor, softly projecting. *I agreed with your course of action, it was the right thing for us to do. We could not have attacked such a force with any chance of success. The sheer numbers they possessed at the time would have overwhelmed us, much as it has happened now.* Kord glanced back over the sea of corpses. *Their numbers are staggering, I fear the Atlanteans have met a similar fate to ours judging by the smoke rising out of their city.*

Takeara found strength for one last desperate telepathic plea. *You must flee, meet up with the matrons and find a new home!* Takeara's breaths grew labored and then they faltered.

I will, but first I have to stop Sagahr and Timmeron. Their bloodlust and conquest must end here. If they salvaged the other ship, they have means to leave the island. Mankind will not be able to stand up to a force such as we've encountered this day. They will dominate everything and no one, including our species, will ever be safe.

Kord craned his long neck back to survey the smoke plumes still rising from New Atlantis. Undoubtedly, Sagahr had gone back to the city to wreak more havoc. Kord took another moment to survey the carnage around him. As far as he could see, smoking, charred corpses of great cats and bears littered marred the landscape. Nearby several more dragon bodies lay – elegant powerful forms violated by tooth, claw and scorched by powerful organic energy beams. The Atlanteans hadn't succeeded in making protectors. Instead, they'd created loathsome, homicidal maniacs hellbent only on death and conquest.

"Hear me Odin, hear me Thor! I will avenge this!" Kord looked down at his fallen comrade, the great elder dragon's pupils had dilated and the once-mighty heart ceased beating. Duncan Kord, last Lord of the Dragons let out a battle roar that carried for several miles shaking the very mountains with its force.

The sun had long set as Kord placed the last stones over the entrance to the dragon cave. He had burned through most of his energy reserves carefully carrying each body home and gently placing it in a dignified position of repose. He placed Takeara on the remains of the massive basalt throne, a fitting resting place for the wise ruler who led his people through so much. He felt tightness in his chest as nausea swept through his body. Then came the horrific pain. Kord knew he'd played out his energy and the amulet was spent. He could not remain in his altered form. He struggled with the transformation back to human. The change gave him a few seconds reprieve before another wave of agony set upon him. Muscles cramped and spasmed. Waves of searing agony coursed through his battered body.

The pain rose to a crescendo, pounding a tortured rhythm through his skull and eye sockets. Kord stumbled, vision blurred by blue sparkles dancing in front of his eyeballs. Each fresh wave of agony dimmed his vision further. "By the gods, am I to die here without avenging my people?"

The Nordic man crumpled, falling face-first into the dirt. In the corner of his eye, he spied his sword. His sword! He hadn't used it since he'd left to search for their new home. He'd forgotten about the weapon safely tucked in his shoulder and wing pocket. The blade had fallen free along with his armor and clothing when he'd changed. Kord painfully crawled toward the weapon, each movement sending shock waves through tortured nerves and muscles. He reached for the hilt but it lay just outside his reach, mocking him. His fingers flexed and stretched but still fell a hand's breadth shy.

"I have failed again. Gods forgive me."

Kord felt the last of his energy wither away. His hand fell limp. Dirt mixed with the tears staining his face as the world faded in and out. The fallen king closed his eyes to finally embrace death. Blackness overtook him as the world faded. His body began to consume itself in a last desperate attempt to feed starving, enhanced flesh. In the myriads of pain and death, the dragon king felt a tingle of vitality shoot through his body.

Kord's eyes opened, each pupil glowing green as more energy invigorated him. His grip on the sword increased and with a smooth jerk of his arm, he unsheathed the weapon.

Emerald white energy crackled up and down the blade as he held the mighty sword over his head screaming out a cry of ecstasy. Pure, unfettered power poured into every energy-hungry cell. A raging torrent quenched the fiery pain he'd endured moments earlier.

"Odin!" he screamed. The single word echoed throughout the mountains of the dragon territory. "By the grace of the gods, I live!"

Kord sheathed his sword and dressed. As he finished buckling his steel breastplate, he sensed a presence hiding in the darkness. The rejuvenated warrior focused his senses. He heard muffled breaths and a rapid human-like heartbeat.

"Have no fear, Atlantean," Kord called out wearily. "We have both lost much this day."

Terrell made his way out of the shadows and approached the dragon lord. The frail being was filthy, his right arm bent in a painfully awkward position indicating a severe break.

"The savages have plundered and destroyed our city. There is nothing left of our civilization but a pile of ruins." Terrell pointed toward the night sky. One of the monolithic towers was ablaze, a lone beacon lighting up an otherwise dark, starless night.

Kord approached the tiny being and gently grabbed the broken limb. "Do not move. This will hurt for a short time but must be done." With a sudden jerk, Kord shifted the broken bones back into alignment. The tiny being gasped in agony. Kord tore off a piece of his shirt and fashioned a makeshift sling for the damaged limb. "I assume your medical areas have been destroyed."

Terrell nodded. "Our library, our meeting hall, and several other buildings have all been set to fire because we could not make weapons for Sagahr and Timmeron. They warned us what would happen if we did not provide them weapons of power." The Atlantean stared at the burning tower. "And they finally followed through on their threat after so long."

"You have no defenses? No weapons of your own? Surely a nation as advanced must..." Kord stopped as the frail being shook his head 'No'.

"The city's defensive systems are in disrepair. We are a nation of scholars and philosophers. Even if we knew how to activate them, the thought of killing anyone, anything, is inconceivable."

The dragon lord shook his head in disgust. "You are a nation of sheep!" he snapped causing the frail being to jump backwards. "Sadly, for you and your kind, Sagahr does not share your virtues. I warned that your scheme would come to no good and sadly I have been proven right. They," Kord gestured toward the dragon cave, now a tomb, "have also paid a high price for your folly. Takeara is dead, our eggs and our youngest hatchlings slaughtered, and many matrons carrying young have been murdered by those butchers. You have placed an entire world in peril. Do you understand that?"

Kord sighed, shook his head and frowned. "It is too late for scolding, Atlantean. I am numb right now. I've lost everything. My brother is dead, many of my brides slain." A tear rolled down his cheek. "My children are all slaughtered, destroyed before they could even take their first breath." More tears fell from his eyes. Kord exhaled and patted the pommel of his massive sword. "I have men and beasts to kill this evening." Kord adjusted his sword as he spoke.

"You haven't the power yet. You are still depleted. The sword has given you enough to sustain you. If you engage in combat, you will only burn through your energy again and collapse as you did when I came upon you. I was able to drag your lifeless hand atop your blade so you could replenish yourself, warrior. I have not the strength to do so again if you are lucky enough to survive more bloodshed."

"Then tonight I will mourn my people. At sunrise I will recharge my amulet and hunt down the tiger and the bear."

Terrell snickered ever so slightly. "There is some justice in the cosmos, dragon lord, for Sagahr and Timmeron turned on each other."

Kord sat upon a nearby flattened outcropping, absently rubbing the mud and tear residue from his face with the back of his hand. "That doesn't surprise me. They are much alike, those two. As former leaders of nations, neither man will be content to be in a subservient position. Eventually they would do war upon each other to establish dominance."

"After they sacked the city, both sides separated. I assumed they were going back to their lairs to regroup and heal. Both men had changed back to their human forms and were near exhaustion. That's when I saw Sagahr slip up behind the Timmeron and try to stab him with a crude stone spear. Timmeron was able to detect the thrust and avoid it. The two fought briefly before they both experienced the same discomfort you endured. A large feline carried Sagahr away and I had heard from another survivor that Timmeron was carried away by one of his bear soldiers."

"Your companion, Saulle, did he survive?"

"Unknown, there are many citizens unaccounted for, assumed trapped beneath the rubble and ruins of our city or in hiding somewhere. Many lay dead in the streets."

"I assume you have a flying craft nearby."

Terrell nodded, gesturing toward a nearby grove of trees barely visible in the darkness. "There, a small clearing behind those trees."

Kord gathered his weapon and carefully lifted the injured being. "I have enough strength to take you home and offer what little aid I can for the next few hours. Then I will settle accounts for my kin."

Duncan Kord, Lord of the Dragons, had never seen such carnage. He absently drew his sword as he walked through the main square. The once-proud, magnificent metropolis had been ransacked. Several smaller buildings had been reduced to piles of rubble, the night skies lit up with the flames of burning towers. Curtains of black smoke often concealed the full moon. Terrell led Kord through a maze of ruined avenues and they stopped frequently to check for life signs from scattered bodies. They found none.

The ground beneath New Atlantis began to rumble and shake. A massive tower off in the distance surrendered to the vibrations and toppled over, vanishing into the darkness.

"A ground tremor," Terrell whispered. The Atlantean was agitated and moved with a panicked desperation deeper into the city. Kord followed quietly while all around him New Atlantis burned.

Terrell came to a large building and struggled to open the heavy metal and glass door. He looked over at Kord. "We must get inside!"

Kord swung his blade into the door, shattering the glass and metal barrier. He cautiously stepped through the jagged opening, absently brushing away several large pieces of glass with his foot. As Terrell stepped through the opening, another ground tremor shook the dying city.

"We must get to the core power unit. I fear we are all doomed!"

Kord followed as they descended into the bowels of the structure. Another tremor shook the entire structure and debris rained down upon them. Kord pushed the frail being aside and swung his blade, deflecting a large slab of stone that could have crushed them both. The stone split and fell away bouncing down the giant stairwell.

"We go to our deaths, Atlantean!"

"No, we are almost there, through that doorway!" Terrell pointed toward a dimly lit corridor.

Kord cautiously followed, expecting the entire building to fall in upon them at any moment. They moved through a series of dimly lit hallways and entered a large control area containing several computer banks. Beyond the control systems was a massive glowing chamber radiating incredible power. A slim being was frantically working a series of controls mumbling in a desperate voice.

"Saulle, you live!"

The tiny being looked up from the maze of buttons and displays. "Our power systems have been damaged by Sagahr's attack. The computers that regulate the geothermal pockets that feed our core are no longer under our control! The system will overload and there is little I can do to stop it!" Another massive tremor shook the complex raining down more debris. "We must leave this place. There is little more that can be done here."

Kord followed the two Atlanteans back up the spiraling stairwell avoiding more falling debris. The sun began to rise and daylight revealed the utter devastation Sagahr and

Timmeron brought to the once proud city. Saulle paused momentarily to take in the onslaught and carnage.

"What have we done? What evils have we wrought this day to deserve such a violent end to our civilization?"

"You played with powers best left to the gods." Kord's eyes followed the rising sun. The dragon lord could already feel his amulet drawing in the first scant rays of light and passing on that power to his weakened body. "You gave power to two barbarian tyrants expecting them to act civilized."

Saulle looked up at the large human, the sadness and remorse clearly etched in his face. "Perhaps, Kord. Our intentions were noble; our results..." he paused looking over the crumbling ruins, "do not reflect our motives."

"The dragons have suffered for your folly as well. My race is all but extinct. Takeara is slain, our nursery destroyed, and many matrons and hatchlings died in the slaughter. The three dragons that remain have fled to find a new home. This is the second time your actions have ruined their existence."

Saulle looked up at the formidable dragon lord. "Take consolation that we will share their fate. Once the power core overflows, it will explode with unimaginable force, blowing a hole through the very fabric of the island, sinking it into the ocean, to be lost like our original home."

Kord was stunned. "When? When will this calamity occur?"

"Before the middle of this new day."

The whole island buckled as another titanic tremor shook the city and the surrounding woodlands. Another tall building toppled, collapsing two other towers as it fell. The impact sounds were deafening.

"We must leave the city and get to higher ground before one of those accursed buildings lands on our heads." Kord turned to leave.

"No!" Saulle replied. "Under duress I told Sagahr of the island's demise hoping his sense of self-preservation would override his need for destruction. I knew once his beams tore through our power facility we were doomed. I had hoped to find some way to control the reactor but it is too late. I fear Sagahr will be actively looking for a way to escape our doom. He must be stopped. If he escapes, all are in danger."

"The ship!" Kord cursed aloud. "Kayanna said they came by ship when they attacked the cave. If he's going to escape, he'll need the ship and that's where we will meet. I'll burn the cursed vessel with him in it if need be. This madness ends here!"

"Go and stop him, Dragon Lord, we will stay here and perish along with our city. Our time has passed. Our civilization is no more." Saulle turned back toward the ruins of New Atlantis. "Nothing can prevent the demise now."

The sun rose higher in the sky feeding Kord much needed energy, healing the multiple bruises and lacerations. Burn scars that adorned his stomach and chest vanished. He was prepared for what lay ahead. Another violent tremor rocked the tiny island. Several more tall, slender towers toppled.

"Go, Nordic King, you cannot save us. Our time has come. The sun will set on the race of Atlanteans. Remember us and remember that our intentions were honorable in all we did despite the horrible traumas we've caused humanity and the dragons." Both tiny beings turned back, walking toward their inevitable doom.

"I will remember you, Atlantean." Kord shed his garments, inhaled a great breath and willed his body to change. Once again, he was a mighty dragon. He looked down upon the beings huddled together as the once mighty Atlantis fell around them. *I will avenge you, and I thank you for the gifts you have bestowed upon me.* With a swift beat of massive wings, Kord was speeding toward the northern shore where Kayanna had suspected the ship was berthed. The sonic boom from his flight shook the morning sky as he sped toward a confrontation with his enemy.

Kord's laser-sharp vision scoured the coastline as he descended. The dragon king prepared his plasma glands and was ready to open fire at the first sight of Sagahr or a ship. Several feline carcasses littered the beach. He circled the area unwilling to land. The creatures were tied together and there was a long, deep drag mark in the sand. Sagahr had used his cats like a team of oxen to pull the ship into the water, the tides had gone out and left the ship stranded. *He used them for burden and simply killed them once the ship made it to the open sea. The self-serving bastard killed his own brethren to save his miserable hide!* Each cat had been eviscerated by energy beams. It was evident that the tiger lord had recovered from his exhaustion.

The dragon king flew out to sea, hoping to spot the fleeing vessel. Despite his fantastic speed, Sagahr had made good his escape in the vastness of the ocean. The ship could have proceeded in any direction, followed any bearing and only a wild stroke of luck would allow him to spot the fleeing vessel. The Earth shook and the skies lit up with a bright orange glow fading into deep mauve. Kord craned his neck back and witnessed a titanic fire storm. New Atlantis erupted, sending chunks of rock, ash and debris miles high into the sky. The dragon realized he needed to gain both altitude and distance to avoid the oncoming shock wave. Large wings cracked like thunder, propelling him forward and higher into the sky. Kord drank hungrily from the amulet burning within his armored chest. It provided him even more power as he winged up and away from the disaster.

Kord sensed that he was now at a safe distance. He executed a perfect aerial loop and hovered ten thousand feet above the ocean. His keen eyes spotted the angry boiling sea and the titanic tidal surge caused by the massive shock wave. Kord hoped that one of those waves or an errant chunk of debris had found Sagahr's vessel and sent it and him to the bottom of the sea to die along with the peaceful race of beings he'd so callously slaughtered. From his point of safety, Kord watched as volcanic ash blotted out the sun even at his high altitude. New Atlantis was gone. All that remained of the island was an angry boiling sea, plumes of black smoke, and columns of hissing steam rising toward a darkening sky.

I am truly alone now, not even an enemy for company. Two families dead and a society destroyed. Damn you to the darkest pit, Sagahr. May whatever gods rule the world smite you for what you've done this day! I will find you, Tiger Lord, and I will kill you! Duncan Kord, last lord of the dragons, turned in the air, hoping to catch a scent and follow the trails of the three matrons that fled earlier. That was his only hope for life.

About the Author

Greg Ballan is a graduate of Northeastern University holding bachelor's degrees in Marketing and Management. Greg enjoys several outdoor activities including hiking, archery and shooting. Greg was an avid MMA fighter but realized after surpassing the age of fifty, getting punched hurts … a lot! He discovered a safer hobby, chasing wildlife with a camera. When he's not working his full-time job as a financial analyst or exploring some unknown woodlands, he's crunched over his laptop putting his warped imagination into words or penning a column about the outdoors or his latest misadventure pursuing the perfect photograph.

Books by Greg Ballan

Lost Sons Series:
Lost Sons: The Fall of New Atlantis
Lost Sons
Lost Sons: The Battle for Manhattan

Hybrid Series:
Hybrid
Hybrid: Forced Vengeance
Battle Lines
Armageddon's Son